For
disobeying

sasha hawkins

DECLASSIFICATION AUTHORITY DERIVED FROM: AUTOMATIC

CONFIDENTIAL

Transmit the following in ___ PLAIN TEXT ___ Via ___ AIRTEL

(Type in plain text or code)

Date:

For disobeying

sasha hawkins

ISBN 978-1-940853-38-3

published by Calamari Archive
NY, NY

TABLE OF CONTENTS

FOR DISOBEYING:

a brief history of production

Bertolucci's *LAST TANGO IN PARIS* (1972)

"in which he's this man, seducing this young woman." [1]

"I've cut the heart out of a living animal before and eaten it while still warm. Totally raw. Still warm… I'd eat your heart if I wasn't stuck without you after."[2]

—RICHARD BRADFORD, IN A PRIVATE LETTER TO MARLON BRANDO (1966)

PREFACE

SCREEN TEST:

"THE MEN" (1950) premiered 25 AUG 1950

ROLE: KEN "FIREBIRD" WILOCEK

CASTING DIRECTOR:

"HE TAKES THE HORSE AWAY, NAKED, AND WON'T LET ME COME WITH HIM."

MARLON:

"I smile over my drink at an unkindness, slick, and seething, and rounding to strong shoulders, turning his drink, closing dream of oliver reed, from a roman afterlife, the filth of the floor, filth of liquor, clutching his chest, it hurts to look good, win, and see yourself with so little, kindness, deliverance, is eating my heart, relieves fevers, divines permits, take any one life on this mountain, he could have anyone, and he calls me pretty, I look around his room, I ask him where he wants my head, he picks me up high like nothing, says it's nothing, really, in his hands, I am, domestic, commanded dog, of war, of pleasure, from one side, above, across, into the quarry, the rocks, cold with me, I get turned on before I have to. he lets me down into his bed.

"I picture myself with someone I love, and the unkindness, having seen us, having contorted me to hold tightest around him, tells this man I fold just like silicone, only I clean myself after, he shows his phone, and the video is genitals, and porcelain, white, rented home, and the men in line, in circles closing in, and their makeup, all bodies dirty, and covering the sun, you don't know if she really likes it, is the deniability, and the excitement.

"she looks at the camera.

"'I prefer not to face them, I wanna do it and all, but that's not how I'm used to taking. my doctor, who sews me up after all this, says it's in childhood when fetish takes hold.'"

"SEND DEEP, SPUR!"

"'she really did love me can you believe it, after the way I fucked her, the way she was scared I'd never go to sleep, she asked me if she could take me to dinner,' I worry it was love, I worry it's always love, forever, the man in his car leaning out, leaning on the horn, a celebration of my pubescence, the exit of eden, my hands on my knees to kiss him, the straps of my bookbag wrenching the shirt up under my arms, words spread thin over me, 'every hard-on // gets you closer to hell,' and a panda for the wwf, if I want it bad enough, you know what you're saying, and you're not saying but asking, and you're not asking but taking my hands away, sliding out the buttons on my fly, I cum, I forgive myself, is all I could do, is drive home to my family, this death as a veteran, fallen to my aging wife, 'if she loves me, well, am I so bad?'

"I TIE THE HORSE HEAD SIDEWAYS."

"I work the muscle to failure, and I lay the skin on top, this man I love, with the bridle, these others run an open palm down me, curving, feeling for imperfections, I had never heard his name before it was his, this man I love, I met two others, in retrospect of his ownership, and possession defined by an absence of vulgarity, a gentle tide, I am a dog snapping at the foam, looking at the sky, my lord, in innocence, ulysses, live with me, always."

"PENDERTON TAKES FIREBIRD FOR WESTERN PLEASURE RIDING."

"you have to believe in the world, and that it's touching you, or else, everything reminds me, snake skin and winding, revolving around a heart, compound eye, a face on its back of surprise, of delight, beautiful man, I've made myself an animal again, a luxury to be stroked, in your bed, begging, if the time was disposable, if it wasn't needed, maybe, I see an unkindness, and he's so angry, 'so what I don't deserve you, when I have you, what do you deserve, and believe in, if not my touch, when I start and end like god, and you leave my hand where I tell you, what you've done, and you'd do to pleasure me, I write, I still have your number, and it's your words, this man you love, does he read?'"

"FAULT! STRIKE!"

"up close with something sharp, as salvation, the

split of raw from living, under the carver, the skin and the fat neat on either side, is the excitement, and what else, so you get it, so what's it matter, this man I love, kept all my notes and trinkets, I wish to be made of their materials, plastic eternal, in his pocket, all along, my father kept our blue shirts, the last time we could fit, the last time we were loved, as children, he encouraged the shed of gentleness, a one-piece bathing suit, a small chest, high necks, long dresses, broad shoulders my father never found desirable, this man I love looks me over, admires all the hard work I do, this look, the breadth, private, and admired, and easy, I get turned on before I have to."

"ROLLKUR!"

[*ALBERT LIZARD, albertosaurus, tore into some guy's guts, some other lesser lizard, or other life, he only knows the world of himself. he eats close to the I-17 sound wall, the expansion out to the gila bend reservation, westward, and taken. his FATHER looked upon the taking with great joy, with fantasies of easy travel to his old lady's place. FATHER told him of life in Hollywood, a place from which he'd moved by his late twenties to have ALBERT and his brothers in quiet, of land, of his mother, of protest toward his desire.*]

FATHER:

these bumpkin girls'll let you do anything. that's the greatest thing I could give you, the totality of a woman.

[*ALBERT was eating the poor sap, some kind of leaf-biting quadruped, and he wished he could change his nature. what FATHER said to ALBERT was less said than called, and grunted out in shrieks. ALBERT understood it, and has translated it for you as, the above. he did not hear it that way. you hear ALBERT as he speaks. his FATHER, loved ones, do not hear it that way. it's this voice in his mouth. he doesn't possess the body for speech, it just rings out from his stomach, and it sounds like paul newman, FATHER says.]*

FATHER:

what a sissy.

[ALBERT was topping off on this guy, about to leave a big mess of his body, and put his head back.]

ALBERT:

I tried to deny myself, but there's nothing in me to prop up the strength. you've got two angels in there and I must know them, lot. I gotta do something about this ache.

[ALBERT imagines the man pleading, grabbing his hard cock, making a ring of the thumb, a horrible, horrible place, where the man puts thoughts of his daughter—oh, if he lost "lot's wife", how could the family go on and on and on to KING DAVID, glorious KING DAVID, pretty for the LORD in his apron, his pretty little apron, tight, and out, and tight, and out, and cum from the man into these girls' asses, and I'd make them stand there awhile, you know, it's a parable. ALBERT brings his head down, hides his guests in the body.]

ALBERT:

please, please, don't do this! please, *please,* I've got daughters even tighter—

ALBERT:

ah, but are they of heaven?

ALBERT:

they are mortal, so shall be your punishment. if you really hurt these guys—who knows what He'll do. the Lord would rather you break the mortal flesh than his divine reserves. haven't you ever had a girl? do you really want to go to hell? you may never cum again–

ALBERT:

I don't remember what he did to me but I remember playing sleep no matter what, I'm asleep, I don't feel the stretch—

[*ALBERT breathes deep into the body, like he's crying. it's unknown whether he really possessed the capability. the AGENT on the other side of the sound wall was willing to take a gamble that it looked as real as it felt. he calls over the wall.*

CLEAR! MARLON. I'D LIKE TO SPEAK TO MARLON NOW.]

AGENT:

I want you to work for me, marlon.

AGENT:

thank you, marlon, please take your seat.

PLUTO ON THE MIDHEAVEN:

I can't stop hurting myself on you. I have lived my life as a difficult man. I'm told it's an abundance of trines, a sort of repeating angle in my stars. I'm too satisfied with myself to—abandon success. throw my little successes to the stop bath. I hold on, and overexpose. I pull god's light out of the sun over everything, a cling wrap sweating you down to weight. your perfect weight, and perfect body screened at grauman's chinese theater. you would sit in the dark an hour. I would give you trailers, and then the dark, and in the dark, you hear your mother worry you're unattractive. and all there is to drink is white claw. I take a sip off the top, and I take a bottle of something clear, cheap, I fill it whole again. and you just drink, and you listen to your mother. and then it's on, and a siren is sounded. you'd trample each other getting out, if anyone could see. if they had ever seen something so beautiful, they wouldn't be locked up like that. if I were a kid again, I'd make that movie. right now, I oughta be in the audience.

but I'm not in the audience. so I guess I'm god? that's really something only you can tell me. you might remember me as sheriff calder in *the chase*. my shirt's been torn. I am thrown down to fine civic wood and the men lock the doors, circle me. rough me up. take turns roughing me up. they sit me upright, tell me what they're gonna do to me. they do me, sit me up again. I don't look like myself anymore. one more time, and I don't feel like myself either. the welts deform the muscle, the physique and show. one more time.

"oh, I can't go anymore," says Richard Bradford, and he wipes himself with his pressed shirt. they're all naked. I'd ripped them clean. this is a poignant moment in my life, the life of those watching. I feel my face, and I can't find my eyes, but still I inspire longing.

"and so mature! so beautiful, and so mature," says Mr. Penn. and I rip myself clean, to show the suffering I've endured, and will endure until Mr. Penn gives the safe word to the crew and all. so, I guess, in a way, that makes Mr. Penn god? people admire Mr. Penn, but they don't know what he looks like, and they don't make guesses about it either. it doesn't fucking matter. no one is painting Mr. Penn, so it doesn't fucking matter. they paint me, the freaks. right before it's safe, Mr. Penn says we must, *must* know how I got here, someone so beautiful, and so mature.

well, nudity is only frightening from certain shots. say Richard holds on to me, in close, my arms stuck down, and when he lets go the bruise will band darkly. I am unafraid. I am dominated, as is the way of things. but if Richard were to come to me, I am dressed and sitting at a narrow table, with his cock at level with my mouth, undressed, I look up at him, I have to look him over to look up at him, he drives conversation. I look away and he drives over to where I am. well, I guess that's fair too! I don't think it can frighten me anymore. and this movie is my dove, light on the air, over seas of my wrath my exhausted patience sails the theater to impossible light.

Richard Bradford was a catholic. Richard Bradford is the dove, with a palm of my hair in place of olives, the white bulb of each strand to be planted upon the docking of the ark.

"let every man have a marlon," says Mr. Penn, or noah I suppose, "and let him feel unclean at the hands of the sower." Richard was the love of my life. on the set of *man in a suitcase*, he'd asked the stuntmen to really give it to him. they'd shaved their hands on him, and made an excellent program. they were hurt, and they'd say no more Richard, and the show would be over. I'd heard that, anyway. I'd lost a sort of virginity to him onscreen, and a week before at his place. he had invited me over. he didn't speak to me much before. he was a real method actor, and closeness, and compassion for my flesh would upend what we set out to film. he could only be my lord. he looks down at me, kneeling on the bed with this strong body, knees in a wide stance. he's put me over his head, I know he's strong. he brought me down close, against him, to let me feel how hard it made him, you know, when I realized how vulnerable I was. I was a little honeyeater. I was the last true honeyeater, in captivity, of artificial rock, glow-paint trees and mongoose. I think of him over me, and I lay out to get cool.

I ask to go to his room. he shared the place with this woman. he was a blond with blue eyes. he's kneeling, and he takes the condom by the reservoir and pulls, tosses it. he's kneeling and I get down in this kinda worship position. this position of service. I'm a real showman. there's only so many ways to take a cock, but I make the memory in little things. he's kneeling, and I'm down lower, taking him in my mouth. I don't cum myself, I never have. I think it's a sort of nervousness. it's a sort of novelty, seeing your cum in someone's mouth. you'd think I was a new shelby cobra the way he smiled at me—god, he was a beautiful man. after everything, I still remember him as beautiful. he tells me I'm amazing. he got cold as soon as he said it. he didn't mean to say it. the love of his life was one room over, and he remembered every second out of the light of his lord was agony. so I guess that makes that woman god. and I can't even remember her name! I was so close to being saved. I think I just swallowed, and he smoked. I think I went home.

here, in the theater, Mr. Penn has called Richard off me. we were sitting there, and he pulled up his shirt to show me he was still beautiful. and he was, after so much longing. in the fear that he never finishes with me is a sensation I'd been lacking. life! I felt life, and I felt it being taken from me. I could really feel my blood. I move on with what I'm left with to west phoenix. I haven't spoken to him in months. I go back to the room, Mr. Penn's room, and they haven't cleaned anything. I'm all over the walls and fixtures. big curtains from ceiling to floor, and at the far left was one hand, and the right was one lower, in red, dried a sort of earthy color. that must be the way everyone else sees this. I meant to ask someone how to reclaim my remains back into my living spirit. it's ruined things for me to lay amongst my golem, but they were perfect for me. maybe my father is god.

Mr. Penn is on another set. who knows what happened to Richard. I wanna know, but he won't speak to me. the cuts have been made. this is going to theaters. you need to start thinking of who to be next, he would say to me, if he'd speak to me. I sit in the middle of the room, and bring my pants down my legs. I play with myself, and I cum remembering how Richard touched me. you don't know it yet, but that's a really sick thing to do. I cum, and the movie ends. like I said, there's no credits. I said that, didn't I? that I don't wanna end things? which is to say, should Mr. Penn see fit, should I feel him again, Richard, with two firm hands wrenching opposite ways, I couldn't help myself. that's why all those people in this book got hurt. I sit up. I clean my hand on my leg, and I know now god looks down on me in the blind.

I'm realizing now, maria, you were no rabbit, you were a woman!

"My dad had been molesting me." [3]

CONVERSATIONS WITH BRANDO (1987)

↑↑↑↑↑↑↑

PART ONE

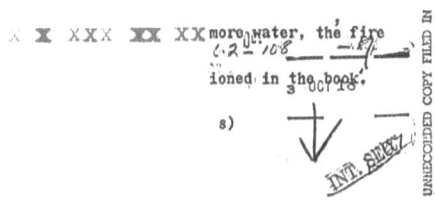

THE TONIGHT SHOW (NBC, 1968)

EXCERPT (1/2):

MB: what hurts the most is I'm baptist. he's pentecostal. he made covenants of fetish. "I promise I'll never get enough of you," he used to preach at revivals. everybody was dying at revivals. they fell to the floor and cracked soft and to collect, to keep the lights on, you take the hook and drive through the belly, and drive in one straight line along the narrow middle. you drive up into the collar and lift, with angels reaching over the hip, the guilt of getting wet lets them down. that's what made it wrong, that you got off too. they give up all they've got after that kind of love, and debasement. a washing joy when he lets your head up, true joy of tested and blessed faith with the end in your mouth. a room to be alone in after.

JC: *is it a political thing? was he trying to get you down?*[4]

it's sinking or diving. it's rehearsed. it's fact. it's an issue of novelty. we'd pack up the tent and let in the sun, the world to turn over. we'd leave them in the field to come back together. push the hook back sticky in our hand. when you press down at the seam it's blinding. they can't be touched anymore. they're good for nothing.

he made me awkward and I held a grudge—

I read a lot of koziński. I've got no shame to me. jerry lee lewis was a fucking pentecostal. I'm half. I'm so tired of myself. I have no empathy for myself. I was looking up if you know when people are looking at you, and if there's a heaven after telling god I want it easy tonight. underneath the perfect will and vision, I push back on his waist. I pull myself up to receive the least of his love, this clenching an issue of the unconditional, unworthiness brings this love. it's red in the white wash, all evidence of reciprocation, under heat, under action, doesn't let me tell him no, or anyone. we're born apostles of his word, mothers second, fuckable most, of everything.

on SCENE ONE, "LAST TANGO IN PARIS—TANGO"

"for disobeying I was a virgin weak in the hands learning to split a girl."

last tango in paris—tango

"I don't wanna know your name!

"not one name.[5]

"out in my garage I've got this machine. I think I bought it with greater fitness in mind, but every time since I first had you, I look at it, and I know just where to put you. that's all that's gonna get a name between you and I. I'll call you up, say it, and you'll come running, and you'll go limping. I wanna strap you to my machine, press you flat to my bed, and with your flinches, and your moaning for worse, receive me. say who all had hurt you, how you cross your legs while being hurt. to have my hand crushed in your denial, and your control in petting down the center of my chest, kissing my shoulders. I felt loved and I got hard. I got on top of you. you wouldn't be wet til after. you never came, almost once. you were loaded and you called it love. that it feels good, lovely animal, to get you clean. make a rug of your back, of the bending spine, tender spur coming apart in my hands, lovely animal. I lay a girl in the skin of your arms. your life isn't worth so much when it's yours. value is dictated by the market. value because it tastes good to feel good. I want you to go home, and I'll get hard again, and I'll send you a picture to open next to your father. or were you the one with the mom. you can show my cock to whoever, as long as you're shy about it. and caught, *imperative* that you get caught. they'll take your phone, you know. you ever get grounded?"

"once," says maria, "when I got bad grades, my mom unplugged my tv and said don't touch it. I left it unplugged a few months. I didn't touch it until she asked what was up with the tv."

"you don't know what you do to me when you talk like that. you couldn't possibly know, or you'd be pretty sick."

"I know."

"you're sick then?"

"I know what you like."

"but you don't get it. you don't really understand what you're saying."

"I never had a room of my own growing up, and I can't cum standing up, so I'd wait until everyone went to sleep and I'd fuck myself in the bathroom, laid out on the opposite side of the toilet and the sink, with my back to the tub. that's the only way I can finish, is on my back."

"have you tried anything else?"

"not with anyone. alone, it's the only way."

"would you try this? I think it'd really get you off:

> a girl is on the bus. the man standing behind her flips her skirt up. his pants come down. we've got similar asses. and I suppose I take after the man. I suppose I was young and growing into it. I would say, yeah, his cock's got a sort of pornstar look to it. it's out, and against her, centered in her ass. she's kind of pushing down on the back of the skirt, and back on his chest. it's more of a pantomime of struggle, and he's kinda swatting her hands away. and once he's in, she can't help but masturbate."

"sure, I could like that."

"I want you to give me three ways in which you enjoyed it."

"well. I enjoy it as someone watching. my father used to tell me how pleasurable it was to be a parent. I find it pleasurable in whatever way he meant, that's two. lastly, you know, I've been fucked on a ferris wheel. I think I could know a little more about this kind of stuff than you give me credit for. in fact, an ex showed me something like this in high school. so I could like it as someone curious."

"I didn't say I liked it. can you imagine the filth on his hands?"

"well—"

"the arizona state fair? tell me you didn't suck yourself off his fingers."

I go over to the mirror, and I look right in my eyes. it does this thing where I'll lose whole minutes. that's really why I don't like them, the sort of pausing effect. it's like sleeping standing up. I get why horses don't live so long in the wild! as long, I should say. they could wanna die. I oughta be nicer to my mother, if I'm assuming everyone wants to live and I know better. he's behind me, marlon, and he's arranged himself on my ass, both hands to keep me pulled to him. I'm not reaching for my pants or anything, but I would say the mirror's a sort of skirt. it's not even that I'm looking at myself, I'm looking at nothing. a sort of *magic eye*. I didn't have those books at christian school, but I've seen infomercials from back when we didn't have cable. tv airs all night, but it also kind of goes off around 2 am. *magic eye*, *zoobooks*, you know, *muzzy*. he starts dragging the ends of my shirt up over my head. I lift my arms and go right back to my skirt. I like the way my breasts look in the hands of someone excited. they want to feel the whole thing. they humiliate themselves all night trying to fit it in their mouth. if only I took pictures! I would never. I like that they can't help themselves, or at least don't know when to. I look at marlon decide where to center his palm. he keeps the nipple out between two fingers, and draws the flesh as inward as it will fold. I would say, if, god help me, we were being filmed, this would be the point where I've given up on the skirt. I've given up on the idea of not being fucked on the way to work. I can't say I know the exact feeling of publicness, but I've known approximations. I really didn't want to fool around on the ferris wheel. you know what, I wouldn't say that. I just wanted to make out. he used to watch a lot of porn, and he'd paid for me to get in, and he was my ride home, and me and my father were not on good terms, and my mother needed to make rent, she's asking *me* to help make rent, I really had no option but to let him put his fingers in my mouth after. I swatted at him awhile too! every ride he was after me. I suppose that's what really works about marlon and I's arrangement. I never see him outside of this place. yeah, he doesn't hear no so good either, but he hears it enough. once, when he was fucking me and really drawing back on the swing, he fell out of me and almost went right up my ass. the way I yelped! I think I said, "wrong hole!" or something, and he said "are you sure?" my heart dropped. I could never watch those videos. I think marlon would search "painal"? I could've cried! I begged, "please, please", whatever, and he just went back to fucking me like normal. ferris wheel guy would've pouted or whatever until I let him fuck my ass dry. he thought, because it's not shown in the tape, lube had no place in the reconstructionist fantasy. "we're filming the take, not the life." in her life, she may or may not have had her ass lubed, but in her take, she has nothing, and she looks it. in the way that I believe bad things should happen to me, it was immensely satisfying. physically, I thought I was going to have to be sewn up. my mom would've been so annoying. so, at least this business with marlon isn't that! another big part of the take is that I get off on the whole thing. I can endure, but to demand I finish is excessive. life under marlon carries no such burden. he never asks me if I came. not because he's so certain, it just doesn't make the mail run on christmas if I do!

on SCENE TWO, "JEANNE"

"for disobeying the girl gets up on the chair and the man pretends to bend down and he pretends to look up and he pretends he's getting hard he tells her thank you for being braver than these other kids thank you for playing with me in condemnation of real lust in exercising real power."

jeanne

I dreamt a hand from above took blood from me, took my flesh. bird down in your fingers. your back laces, body stilled in exhale, I dreamt I held open your fucking mouth. you smile against my fingers. you can't contain your joy. it comes down your chin, oh god. oh fuck, I was close. you left cuts in your wet skin, the pink of your mouth, your lip folds over your teeth. you chew yourself up to keep me safe. oh god, you could be my mother. you'd probably let me call you mommy, that's what keeps me on top of you. if I told you I liked foot stuff, or ass stuff, the very next visit I would have it, and well. you'd be practiced. if I asked you to make me a costume for the christmas show, you'd make it, and I wouldn't be afraid to ask. I could ask you early, and we'd really make something nice.

you know, I'll admit, the first time was alright. I didn't *need* to see her again, I'll tell you that much. she talked her way over with promises of no-holds barred action. she's kept her promise as well as anyone from the suburbs can. it's not about depth of play so much as earnestness. that she wants me to cum so bad. and I want to, but I want this to last. I wanna see what new noises you'll make to praise me, mommy. I ought to just say it. she's a real freak for volume when I finish. she won't eat it or nothing after it's cold though. she says it makes her nauseous. she's spit such beautiful snow. she's hasn't seen snow in her life, but she knew just what I liked about it. she knows me. when I punish her for knowing, she understands. she comes over next week if I invite her. she's asking to come either way. on top a fitted sheet, this bed and carpet bawling, I'm sweating onto you with jealousy like spit all over. I, too, wish to be destroyed. I'm all alone if I really get you off. I wanna know all about you. I want you to know all about me, then we'll talk about whatever it is she wants, and how close I can get her. I made the other girls do more. I don't regret that. I feel it's brought me patience enough to really get somewhere with her. farther than I've ever gotten with a girl, and it's over nothing. I don't even need a tape running when we fuck, I'm done just looking at her. I'd like to take you all the way, animal bath, make me a new mother. make me a child and let me try again.

on SCENE THREE, "GIRL IN BLACK— TANGO (PARA MI NEGRA)"

"for disobeying he straightens the hand and strikes and gropes at my flat body but I love my father? is it cold in here? do you have a different top? can you come in from the pool with us girls? can you come talk and show through everything hot or cold see me and dream the failures of decency, so much power over the weak."

girl in black—tango (para mi negra)

my bit?

I'm the principal begging her not to turn me on. her legs finally shaping into a woman's, her clothes from the juniors' section, she couldn't stop hurting herself. she tells me it's all happening like she read and watched. home alone with showtime, the little girl wonders is he all that bad if it turns her on, too, witnessing his power and his sex. no one's talked to her about it, assuming she knows about it. I've seen what she watches. next time I tell her father what I've walked in on.

she was clueless when I picked her up. I asked her how she'd tried to get off. she said she took her own two fingers, and waited on the thrill. she got her lip gloss, a stout little guy. she left the door open and fucked herself, again, waiting on the thrill. if it were bigger, if she felt herself barely holding—you can't teach curiosity. I wait until she gets in the house before I leave. it's like real care. it's like a real movie. the way her father comes out and poses, it's like real care.

unafraid of my cruelty, envious of my natural right to be pleasured endless by the perfect girl, she dreams about me. I've said things to her so-called women couldn't take. you know, and she might be naïve, and think she can satisfy me for good, but you can't teach fetish. she would make the perfect kid. I'm too coward to raise my own. I'm too hard to tell her she's sick and turning, help me god, I'm scared she'll send me to hell. oh god, when I'm over her, the reflection, and the eye, the golden eye gets wide to fit me!

on SCENE FOUR, "LAST TANGO IN PARIS—BALLAD"

"for disobeying my lover wouldn't even look at me before we got started my lover goes to the knuckle and twists and talks soft right through the skin over my heart an admittance of unworthiness of me bare and smiling and taking my lover in my mouth 'so I'm not good enough for gold,' says my lover, arms wrapped around the back of my head I can't push for nothing or breathe for nothing exciting my lover my savior clearing my throat my savior almost the excitement of re-entry looks at me pulls up behind me in a beat sedan and goes slow, waving, handsome."

last tango in paris—ballad

"ain't I pretty?

"ain't I desirable?

"don't I lift?

"ain't I big, god?"

"as much as read."

"your quarry goes to ground, am I to go after it?"

"paw at the cold dirt. lick it, get it hot again, get her ready, and take the den from the top. you are both my children. my cock is tucked up into my waistband. salve my skin of her fight. the undeniable relief of satiated need. the world is a worthless place, look how it breaks apart to sheets. I remain whole. your mother couldn't even do that. she's in the dirt somewhere with her sissy little boy. oh, get her ready. we will eat famously tonight. before this bounty, I was losing my wife. I really was. I'd moved into a two-bedroom apartment. my mother slept in one room. I had two kids who'd share a bed. most times with each other, sometimes with me. we moved a year or so later to another two-bedroom. my daughter would stay up so late to get out of sleeping with me. she figured if I knocked out early in the bed she'd just stay out on the couch. I pay the rent. I send you to bed, and it happens, right? I get another two-bedroom. I start seeing a young lady who'd like to fix my kids. I buy a house, and I have her over. three-bedroom, two bath. my mother in one room, my kids share the other. I've only got the one bed in there. she sleeps on the floor. what a girl! what a skin. she moves down to the living room couch, and she never wears a bra. I'm up early before she can fix her sheets. she's well-endowed, she can't help herself. why would a fox set up shop in my living room, of all places, and be so shocked by the hunt, you could ask. somewhere on the way to me, they taught her to stop flinching. imagine my surprise when she crawls on top of me to die, her small eyes straining to see the kindness of the saving dark. the sun with its face up to the trees. he's just a little boy inside. he's never seen anything like you, show a little compassion. he sits on his hands, his crying and his spit along the side of his face, along the linoleum dark with filth, fall, honeycomb, open to honey."

on SCENE FIVE, "FAKE OPHELIA"

"for disobeying she's had her eyes licked she pulls out the hair on her pussy trying to get clean re-entry pulls up behind her and goes slow she runs and the car runs after, gripping, handsome."

fake ophelia

oh reflection. oh golden eye, I get so angry. I don't listen
so good. there's a man with his arms in mine and he
makes me kill. he makes me eat it. eating, properly eating,
even under duress, is key to the kind of acting I do. my
grandmother would wash the dishes herself long after the
senses had begun to decline. an issue! I was given a sort
of neat-freak label for how close I'd check the plates. it's
not that I wouldn't eat off them, I would, but I would
clean the prongs of the fork the rest of the way. the base
of the prong, where it curves into the next, was a real
problem area. I'd clean it the rest of the way, and she'd
ask me what I was doing. I'm at the sink, and she asks
what I'm doing. I was a very dull child, and I assumed a
sort of dullness to the world around me. I think she just
doesn't get it. "it just had some stuff on it," I said.

"just leave it in the sink and get a new one."

"this one's okay."

"you just said it was dirty. I'll clean it later," she said.
now, you and I know the next fork isn't going to be any

better. for that role, I felt that eating from the tip of the
fork would suit the character best. I was still to enjoy the
meal. compliments, and remarks are a must. and she was
a fabulous cook. a good eye for cuts of meat. just like
if a character were happily married, or loved by either
parent, I would need to leverage my previous experiences
of joy, of almost any kind, into the reading, rather than
pulling from this set, this thing the woodworkers threw
up. I'd had a clean fork before. I loved orange juice, and
the cups were allowed to be rinsed before use, depending
on her mood. I then became a sort of juice-freak around
the house, and I realized the home is a sort of set. I was
saying earlier that home is an experimental shoot. you
could be making anything. under the director, I imagined
myself as the perfect daughter. that's what they all wanted
out of me. the object of the film was to straighten out my
expectations, both received and called towards. we were
making something completely new. anyway, you'd asked
me about acting. that role prepared me for many of life's
filmic techniques. my mother loved this little hole-in-the-
wall in the arizona mills parking lot. it was a large trailer
fabrication, that inside was a *happy days* kind of theme.
a diner. she was nuts about it. the music, the food, the
get-ups they put the staff in. the place was a chain with
the feel of a dive, the hygiene of a dive. a field cricket
the length of my ring finger crawls out from beneath the
bar. we're at a booth across. the waiters step around it. in
fact, I'm the only guy eating that's noticed it. I don't want
to be a hassle. there was lipstick on my water already. I
wasn't a hassle over that either, I just turned the stain

away from my mother. I just drank right next to it. don't pay for acting school, come over for dinner! you come out for dinner right fucking now. my mother will tell you what you're worth. you know, and I could be paul. I'm never certain what year it is, but I understand my capacity for cruelty, and the permanence of personality. no one's tried to arm a rabbit though, so I can't say for sure. what if it worked! it'd be kind of flattering to be hunted. he asks why I won't eat then. well, if I had to say for certain, I'd say what's wrong is you never made me feel valuable. I get the impression that if I died and was made into your trinket, it would have a crass purpose and a matted texture. you'd never ask your lover to take her shoes off before she stepped on me.

am I marlon or am I maria? both my parents are straight. I can't speak for maria. no, I'm mistaken again, I don't know that my father turned down anything. I can't speak for maria's father. neither of us responsible for these urges, the urge to kill and be killed natural. desire eats us all in time. I don't wanna wait out here in the rain for her to figure out what mouth she wants to be in. I know it's mine. I know mine is as good as any. consumption is consumption is consumption is these clouds coming in dark against the black. I convince her she can't go home, she'd never make it.

on SCENE SIX, "PICTURE IN THE RAIN"

"for disobeying lot took me to the cave."

picture in the rain

golden eye, reflecting a dirty theater:

the first tape you ever showed me was in my cousin's boombox. there were about eight kids living in a three-bedroom house, which, with bunk beds, meant a bed for everyone come the harvest of tax season. in leaner times, the room count remained static, but rental furniture was lost. the oldest boy had a cd player, amongst a handful of other personal belongings hidden away in laundry, a prayer for privacy and a sacrifice to nourish it's body. and us kids went through everything. we needed hiding spaces. we played a game in which one of us would play the mother, the others her children, and we would pretend to sleep, and the mother would beat us, more often than not, with a clothes hanger. it was an exhilarating game at the time. and mother would only stop because she'd get a little bored of hitting and wanted to be hit. us kids would rotate roles, but I almost always played a kid, by choice if you can believe it! I've always loved being hurt. anyway, I'm making a break from mother's house. I'm hiding in a closet, up to my waist in stiff, soiled clothing, having the time of my life. escape is the ultimate bogart of attention. we'll at least have to stage a child-to-mother intervention, where the kids beg their mother to stop spanking me. I would consider this the climax of the storytelling of the game. anyway, I'm in this laundry, and I pop open this cd player by accident. it's got some dirty movie in it. the cover is a woman in a gold lamé swimsuit top, a small, triangular cup, with open legs. you can tell by the forward flat of the hip she's got nothing on down there, but the center plastic's been punched out. the plastic bit that keeps the cd on the player is where I'm told the genitals are. I don't know how long I stared at her. I can't think of her without smelling that closet. mother's been wailing on the kids a while now, and the rest of the house has grown weary of the noise.

"where's marlon?"

I wade out of the closet. the oldest boy watches me cover back up the boombox, his boombox in fact. we were getting pizza later, and my father was paying, so he'd just have to get over it.

at dinner, thinking about how bad I want back in the cd player, folding my legs up on the chair, my heel up against my excitement, I remember she had a cross of electrical tape over each tit. I think it would be scenically inappropriate for me to be so aroused in the moment, what with my commitment to the ongoing project. this project-between-projects. this one-man passion project. the verdict: unremarkable, but crucial to his growth as a performer (love mom and dad).

I can't take any more guilt. I can't eat like this. consequence, sit with me. bleaching, tightening consequence, sit with me, pump a little harder. be my lover, with three fingers inside. it could be my hand stretching you, consequence, and making you feel good. I'm at the top of the stairs, in awe of her crawling. her back bright, ridged, flexing, from hip to hip. my dream held down under me until nothing comes from my cock anymore. I'm worried my chest could be any in her hands. if I film it, the permanence of my body, her face all far away, there's no question of pain in theaters. I live each moment in three big colors: staining, stained, and to be stained.

XXXXX X XXX XX XX X XXXXXX

PART TWO

THE TONIGHT SHOW (NBC, 1968)

EXCERPT (2/2):

MB: everyone has accidents. and I could've just not answered, and not have come around anymore. my doctor was talking about disability, I was so out of it. it wasn't projected that I'd be able to support myself. and for a long time, I didn't, you know, and he helped me out then, he just made me not want it sometimes. just to save a talk, or an accident. I don't know what I'm talking about.

JC: *well you said you were a willing participant, and business is hard.*

it's why I see doctors so much. I get these thoughts and have these fears. you know, sometimes, it's like I've got nothing to do in this life but be sick. I was raised baptist. the church had green seats, felt like carpet on my face. the baptism pool had this window, this scratched plastic cornered by white plaster, white metal. they prayed my young flesh be renewed even younger, even purer. wet white shirt, without a bra, with only panties, with hands to hold his, or hold me in. business is hard all over. a bra and panties, just listen to me. sometimes when I'm writing, and I'm telling you what's wrong with me, I feel like I'm the girl.

were you forced to?

I was forced to be a man, you could say that, but it's not force so much as order, and I've told you all about the order of things. I was coming up to Richard's place. it was a while after we've met the first time. it's maybe the third time we've met. it was this mirror, where god knows what he's watching—you ever hear of gooning? it's what they watch, and I'm watching this—stuff, it's bad, I don't even wanna say. I'd always tell myself it wasn't real, what's happening to this woman, but I have an eye for artifice. I can only get hard with real cinema. the cold people around a tv, "this is sick, and we're sick for making it, like god for selling, or jesus for burning tapes." and he has a fight with the woman he loves, and he calls me over, young, looking even younger. we go quiet to his room. he says he's angry. I take off all my clothes in the light. he looks at me and he smokes, then he gets naked, or maybe he's got his boxers on. we kiss a little, but he's already hard. and maybe he pulls himself through his boxers. I think he's big, but he's shy about it. he tries to fit himself in normal condoms, a sort of highwater effect, but we never got to talk about why. this can't be put off any longer. so he shapes me on the ground, on my knees, facing away from him. he puts his palm between my shoulders and presses forward and presses down. I'm pinned, not that I want to get up, not that I'm fighting. he can see in my face I'm not gonna fight. I couldn't fight, and he squats down, and puts himself inside me, and goes at me. the world's on its side. he's got this mirror standing on the floor, where I can only see my back, my ass high, and him looking down at me. I'm trying to hit my beats, you know, and trying to make the noises I'm supposed to, but it hurts. I can't think of the scene, I'm hurt so bad. it's like we're fucking on a tv remote. I'm a french teen, and I'm Mr. Penn. I'm so small against him. I was always censured for my tonnage, and the caps on my shoulders, but I'm realizing now my mother has no idea what she's talking about. she knows nothing of manhood. I look like a woman against him. I'm anyone with pressure. "I've never been hurt like this," I think. I try to really keep the taste of pleasure in my mouth, but it's too sweet. it makes me nauseous. it's like dimetapp. it was bought with my experience in mind, such care, right in the gut, through wet, bored tunnels. I wish I could see his work inside of me. I wish for benches, for you all to come sit and admire me, my short film installation, on the mechanics of orgasm. my bravery and my tolerance detailed in character sketches, drawn while smoking, while sending me dirty letters, outlines of what's to be suffered, exciting us both, the craft of met needs. I thought it was what I needed. my discipline on a monitor. a man gets dressed for work and watches us like the weather. he shuts us off when his wife comes in, and he sits in his basement getting the nerve to act, to go to work or go to his woman. I rub my face in the floor for this man, his fumbling at the humanity of young partners, intimate with the body, and he, worse, and loud, pictures himself a knife, cleaning me, and, finally, punishment. the cruelty of the world is sewn the look of stamen, full grain skin against the pistil, births a holster, births a sheath, screaming, like they could never hear one another. abandon, in a dream, with only what's wrong with you to stand over and cum on. "it's sick, it really is." Richard rests over me, shuts me off, end of tape, the staging of bodies to imply intimacy, and intention, and the guilt, the guilt. "I watched the whole thing," shutting off the computer. washing the smell of your body from your hands. he's out of breath. I go to be held, Richard says don't touch me. he says he needs a second, he can't be touched right now. I lay on the other pillow, at the other side. he says he's sorry, because—I didn't get this—because he'd lost himself to arousal. he frightened himself! I say no, I had a good time! no, I had fun.

on SCENE SEVEN, "RETURN—TANGO (LA VUELTA)"

"for lot I keep the outfits he likes and when I'm alone oh man all I am is pretty I hit myself and I leave bruises and I leave knots I bite my hands til they don't work I get lost and I think of being hurt hours I get lost and I dream it's me and him in the tunnel of love faking were pedestrian missionary it's fantasy it's life in his mother's head of endless glory."

return—tango (la vuelta)

the golden eye is a moon over water.

just remember to come down sometime. be with me, baby. stay home with the kids. I do great for myself. I'm reading great things. kosiński mostly. I read *steps* at inpatient. I read *blind date* once you'd left me. I read reviews to tell me it's alright to like it, to feel something by it, the terribly erotic. sex as a horror. what would you call this becoming? this outfit decompensating? I hesitate in my eyes, my body forward after your hand from the dark. can't you feel me? I'm so excited. we can't help ourselves, I'm certain. I look like I'm a boy from heaven, I'm certain. cry over me, make a mistake.

on SCENE EIGHT, "IT'S OVER"

"for lot I was a dumb black whore fucking bitch I was so bad when I was little I beg him to keep it a secret he played with my tit in front of everyone he says pray if you don't want anyone to hear about it I do it in a mirror I sit on my heels and curve my back to best please him my lord watching my lord gave up skin for something better."

it's over

under a golden eye, I'm happy to watch her in love from every window to the same room, bright inside, dark outside, besides her light, I kneel. I open my legs. I could be someone you love in shameful ecstasy. I could put on your silly hat, and wear this sweater like a dress. it could be your hand making me your girlfriend, golden eye, make me your little girl. you would see that you cannot help yourself in such a situation. if you saw you, you'd get it. and I'm not saying this from a chauvinistic place, I've been the victim of men same as anyone. you ought to see pictures of me growing up. my mother told me I was quite the smoke show growing up. "what happened?" she asks, and waits for my answer. having shared it, it is now time for her to share her answer with me. "I think you got too much attention for your body, and now you're hiding it. you're insecure about your body, which is just silly to me seeing how I've always praised marlon's body, its size, its muscularity is what I dreamt of having growing up. he's so modest about it. there's a way to show yourself without being fast or whatever. I was never fast, but I could dress. I got my attention fair and square. all marlon does is roll up his shorts, and it's just a real attention suck. I worry about him. people that look like him don't grow up to be good people." and I haven't. it's why I'm out here in the garden, golden eye, I never learned to respect women's boundaries. she'd wear her bra around the house. "this is how they're supposed to fit, it's good that you know." I always wanted to learn chess. no one got around to teaching me.

on SCENE NINE, "GOODBYE (UN LARGO ADIOS)"

"for lot likes it when I crawl and bare and smiling and taking my lover in my mouth he marks it white and his own possession noted only by the lord by perfect vision seen and seen a gift a bowl made from my lips looking in my only excitement the books do nothing praise is nothing looking in proud of me wanting me around I feel like god's special girl."

goodbye (un largo adios)

being watched in a mirror.

keeping my mouth soft. idle eyes in a downturned head, and otherwise, and otherwise: fantasy formless. downturned head like a dog, my whole fist in my mouth. what's enjoyed of me, core tenets of life. to be a true imitation of life, one specific life limited solely by cost, and dreaming. to be with you, and smile, and sing for you, sitting there, doing nothing, the center of your eyes and turning head getting so drunk.

on SCENE TEN, "WHY DID SHE CHOOSE YOU"

"for lot I don't know what he wants I don't know what he dreams I don't say no to love I make myself small for love he demands of me and he pushes me I'm afraid he's in the vents what's the point of all of this if I don't get what I want when I get naked my mom didn't know it was so bad I didn't either dogs weren't people then."

why did she choose you?

lay down in it, the proof of god's existence and favor
toward me.

it's not really night. that's why it's blue instead of the dark,
golden eye. he lays us on our backs into the still bank and
says wait, don't you get up, not even if the blood of the
lamb rushes, not even if the blood shows mercy and I will
show you better. after death, in itself nothing, the courage
in your heart, the brain in your head, are taken up like
air in the lungs, the sinuses. it's invigorating to be so near
you. it's home, black and white. it's simple stuff to be with
you, heaven allowing, heaven stopping me from tearing
you apart.

on SCENE ELEVEN, "LAST TANGO IN PARIS—JAZZ WALTZ"

"for lot I turned around and looked at him and he looked right at my hot hot body he looked down all shy and he looked up at my big big breasts he tells them he's sorry and he asks to see all the clapton we've got I know you've never been to heaven just like everyone else I don't remember restraint shown or living like a child but I put on pants like you little people I don't tell stories like they happened I've just got this ass and these tits and this face is all."

last tango in paris—jazz waltz

I won't talk about the eye again but I'm scared of him. these fences only cover half the yard. the houses all face different ways. fathers, contractors wishing different ways about themselves, changing nothing. kissing houses in need of rubbers, more children. is a house a parent? can a house be dangerous that way? yes! it's not enough rooms. if anyone would come over and count, things would be different. he would've had to answer, I'm guessing, it changes nothing. knot the belt. I've got a canopy bed, I don't have to go to the fan. loop the belt. on my knees in worship of girlish suffering, naked, woven wide, the belt turns up my chin. I look my savior in the eye and beg for release, I'm close, god, let me finish.

on SCENE TWELVE, "THE LAST TANGO IN PARIS SUITE"

"for lot I got upset and I said if the gun was there I'd do it heavy in a plastic drawer and meant to be the dark ride the tunnel of love bored right through the mouth and when I lick at the gate the post the slits the cut will be sweet polite understood the clip was gone and I laughed!

I saw him the next day :)"

the last tango in paris suite

heaven allows wandering hands and heaven allows the same accident a hundred times without saying sorry. without keeping special movies, they don't even know it's happened. if you can resist vanity, peeled labels, their skin doesn't tear the same. golden eye, I just wanted you so bad I can't even cry anymore. I can't even cum anymore. is it really so scary? perpetual release? unending pleasure? just like sleep? being touched in your dreams it can be whoever, a violence in reflection, intimate in practice, staining, skinning, and giving new life to the cover on a new body. a new kind of love for you, golden eye, and if we were aligned so by the divine as a trial, speak to me his word. I believe this to be a satisfying conclusion. I believe the word to be: "that god understands my intentions, that the body is erotic, and yours oh man! your eyes looking up at me mean it. I guess you oughta say sorry too."

"And I just fired every shot I had. I didn't stop to take a look at what I was doing after each shot. I just fired until there was nothing left."[3]

CONVERSATIONS WITH BRANDO (1987)

OUTTAKES

++++++++++++++++
++++++++++++

paul finds the body

"I'm sorry, I don't know why you did it"[5]

he stands over his father, holding a board with five drawn boxes. they are how marlon sr. is to speak to marlon jr.

"they told me you didn't mean to hurt me. I wonder what you thought would happen. how I would change. the sweat pours. hands going long and through the lovely couple means nothing to me. I'll eat anything, and I'll put on my skirt the same. in the wind, unafraid to bend, and show me, he didn't aim to hurt me, but it didn't matter so much if he did. to him, and for me, I'm not a playground so much as a dog caught by boys to whom life doesn't mean so much, owned by others who don't give a shit where you are. the husband stands at the table, over his son and his daughter.

"wives owe us a long life, impeccably cooked, a dog I can stand.

"slaughtered by their sons, poorly, provider, caretaker, red at the corners of the mouth, rolling out cuts of bone, take up the meat, reject the bone," the father has both boys by the back of the neck, sliding against the direction of the nape, touching such sensitive skin. "look how the sensation draws the arms up into the chest. you are resisting yourself for me and the feeling is indescribable."

marlon's father looks over the boxes. the occupational therapist worked with him to design an analog hotkeys set-up, each cardinal direction, and intercardinal direction, a decisive answer to any question he may come across.

she told me, "things like this normally take years to scheme out. people are so complex. what is that, eight answers to every question you could come across? our detractors say it's nothing more than a glorified magic 8 ball, because we do not believe those unable to speak deserve to make decisions for themselves. that, because they are now disabled, there is this added expectation of virtue. now he's gotta be a good guy? no! now he's gotta find a new way to be himself.

"when you look at men like him, who've got what it takes—this man has been cycling testosterone since before marlon jr. was a twitch in his ball. this guy was racing with future olympians. from what I'm told this *marlon* kid could stand to learn a little something from mr. brando. it's been an honor working with him on this. I would love it if he would now pick a response for our flattery."

mr. brando looks at the center of the figure, then—

"northwest!

"he says, 'marlon, I'd really like it if you bathed me.'"

"is that an interpretation of the direction—"

"that's a direct translation of the instrument."

"may I see the instrument?"

"you're a real control freak. mr. brando told me what a freak you were, but I couldn't believe the extent. mr. brando, response? northwest, again, you really ought to get to it. and another thing: west. west? oh mr. brando, what a flirt you are!"

"I'd like to finish my story."

"you do whatever you gotta man, but I'll see to it northwest happens. I won't let you kick this man around like you kick everyone else. yeah, that's right, I've met your mother too. do whatever you have to, sicko."

I used this moment to prep for the scene in which I clear the table in *streetcar*. I pictured this doctor served on the cloth. I would say I made my mother stella, and my father blanche, and the china under the teacup was the flesh pulped and foaming, because of the pressure, because of the spit.

I go outside the hospital down to the street. I sit on the train. I'm crying because I don't wanna die, I just don't see nothing else. I get home. I get upset when the women stop getting hurt.

I watch my shadow onscreen. I prayed to god and I believed myself to be answered. I'd grown a passion for making men money, and being close to you. I would've done anything you would never. I wonder—I think if you met me I'd be scared, and when you fucked me I'd go limp, then, after, I don't know where am I. I think we met when I had a lot of power. that's why it's okay to cum thinking of you, the one true song of my eyes, and its overlays terrible noise, 19 songs about, you know, you never really know someone besides doing, and saying.

a bottle can't tip itself without the delusion of exclusivity, of humanity. in this program I'll lose my wife, I'll lose my sons, I'll be castrated, meaningful pain, inexcusable, that nobody takes up for.

the father's got a finger down the back of his son's collars. the wife stands at the table, over his daughter.

"you are to be wed soon. you need to get a taste for making *someone* around here happy," says the mother.

"Do U promise to make me proud Baby? Will U show him what a porno star u can be? Will U show off for me like never before????" [6]

MARLON BRANDO, SR., IN A
PRIVATE LETTER TO MARLON
BRANDO (1965)

PERSON TO PERSON (CBS, 1955)

S2.E34 (aired 4/1)

featuring actor Marlon Brando and his mother Dorothy Brando

DOROTHY:

that otter's a man, he ought to know better! *who* would *rape* a *baby otter*? they look like *babies*, a definite no go for me, guy. it definitely doesn't turn my engine. they're not even *hot*, it's just *wrong*.

MURROW:

if they were hot?

DOROTHY:

you know, and I have been in that situation, having a *really* hot kid, I just say, do what you can. you try your best to guide them, but they're always gonna think they're a normal kid. it never gets easier to correct.

DOROTHY:

such an angry kid. takes after his father. I always tell marlon, "I will always love your father." then he'll dredge up some horror story. I just look away, and let him compose himself. I do what I can, and I understand him like no one else, he just—rejects love. that's always been the problem between us, and between his father. you'd think he was being beaten this whole time, the way he recounts things! his father only put his hands on marlon once. I told him it was going to happen, him being either, actually, nobody listens to me! I said "marlon is getting out of control." he was always coming home with some new toy, and some bad attitude. he'd ceased all bathing while over his father's house. the smell turned my stomach. I'm sensitive to smells, so it was particularly overwhelming for me. but yeah, he reeks, and the attitude reeks even worse! he's flinching every time I go to kiss his cheek, like he's nauseated by me. his father tells me I'm jealous of their relationship. yeah, alright. marlon gets mad, and he kicks the guy. he loses it. no blood or anything, just a spanking. and it wasn't over the lap, either, he just had him up high by the wrist. everything was above the board, just how I told him it would happen. anyway. marlon goes off to his grandma's room. I guess he slept on the floor a lot of the time over his father's house—

MARLON:
if I had a say—

DOROTHY:
why wouldn't you have a say? if you had your say, you would sleep on the ground? because you're too good to share a bed with your brother?

MURROW:
was it just your brother, marlon?

DOROTHY:
who else would be there?

MARLON:
it's not right to keep teens out in the open. it's like you're asking to see something—

DOROTHY:
marlon, your father doesn't think of you that way.

MARLON:
demanding to see something—

DOROTHY:

I'd like you to stop implying so before I have to *make* you stop.

DOROTHY:

in fact, I can make a lot more stop than that! marlon's never had to fight for anything, I have! *we* have! people like him get everything.

AUDIENCE:

applause.

DOROTHY:

I couldn't give them much, but I always gave them a bed! he didn't tell me until he was on his own, just to throw it in my face, I guess. his father called me crying. sobbing! he was seeing some woman at the time, I'll add! "oh, I hit marlon! how could he do this to me?" did I tell you marlon kicked him first? they were playing some game— marlon would go *nuts* when he lost! a little ribbing and he would be in hysterics. his father was always quite the comedian. he would throw marlon into fits, poor boy. his father never grew up, unfortunately. his mother was a cruel lady. she would lock him in the garage when she'd go to church, and his uncle would bite at the big door, the pull-down door, for hours. and marlon thinks he's had it rough. anyway, I laughed when I got the call. I thought the whole situation was a hoot.

MARLON:

which is to say, the man otter and the child otter become vulnerable populations. one thing you must never ever do to the vulnerable is break down their passion. they'll die without it, and then you, mrs. brando, without him. that's where the woman otter comes in. I won't say she *let* anything happen. he was most unnatural of everyone there, this man otter. once we were all in bed together, my mother, my father, and I. I think I was less than a year old. I fell out of the bed onto this decorative trash can. it sliced right through my forehead. they said I cried or shrieked a while. we waited in the hospital lobby so long I overcame it. I went around the room, to the sick masses of the room. I put my hands on their lap and said

MARLON:

"hello! my face is coming off. they told me the surgeon's a real magician. I'm here for a refund! no, I'm joking, you're gonna be just fine. they haven't healed me yet, but they will. and you won't be able to tell past the body. everyone's gonna love my body. yeah, you have a good one!"

MARLON:

"hello! will you hold me? my mother is in hysterics, and my father must tend to her. will you tend to me?"

MARLON:

they're nice to me. the disgust with my body, the very thought of providing it comfort was a tending in itself. I held no hard feelings at the time either. if it were happening any later in life, it may have made me feel ugly. we don't have anyone after babies.

MARLON:

"a severely underbaked cake. or maybe a cake without eggs. and some people like it that way, but it's not for me."

MARLON:

it's still undercooked. it's still gotta keep some excess of moisture about itself. I would ride the bus home to catch the *law and order svu* marathon on usa network. I didn't quite know how to masturbate yet, but I would become aroused. it got me thinking about how to. I didn't know who I was, metaphorically, in a penetrative sense. I'd only had fantasies one way before, as the assaulted actor, but I think that having the fantasy, seeking out the likeminded and the things they're moved to make, tuning in, I don't watch anything else but *the simpsons* at 10 pm, 10:30 pm, *cheaters* at 11:30 pm if I could swing it, I think by indulging fetish, and trauma play, I became, say, dominant over the image, he acts, and he tells him to, but I am what makes this business successful. I went from lap to lap. the doctor sees me. my mother says

MARLON:

"but doctor, see me!"

MARLON:

she's lost everything, and she can't take care of herself. he holds a stethoscope to her heart, pressing across the chest, back across the chest, across the chest, my father watching, my face pressed in place by sterile latex, by some passing parent who'd felt bad for me and never cared much for their own kid. a tough kid like this, and I'd—

MARLON:

chest of the doctor and the doctor's light, another tending. my father's back to me the greatest.

DOROTHY:

oh, I suppose you slept on the floor once or twice over my grandmother's, a year or two at the most. remember we had seafood and watched steve harvey's *don't trip, he ain't through with me yet?* we had our own premiere party, and I let you eat in front of the tv! how fun was I? they don't know, marlon and his brother, how dire things really were. I was a single parent, and I was underwater. I was borrowing cash from marlon, times were so rough. I never asked their father for a dollar more than the state ordered. even after they said it wasn't fair anymore, I did things on my own, with help from my boys, of course, and I do thank you, marlon.

MURROW:

marlon, what do you want to say to your mother?

DOROTHY:

look at me, marlon. I know you hate it, but we've got to be honest with each other. thank you, marlon.

MURROW:

and your face in her hands, marlon, looks like everything should. and you say

MARLON:

you're welcome, mom.

DOROTHY:

I always tell marlon, when you hit it big, and I just know he will, he hasn't hit it just yet, but he's gonna with any picture now, I tell all my friends how beautiful marlon is, I tell the girls—I say

DOROTHY:

"marlon, when you make it big, I just want 5k and I'll be set and I'll be on my way."

DOROTHY:

5k and I'll never ask again.

EXCERPT FROM A STREETCAR
NAMED DESIRE (1951)

Identity

-11

T-12

T-13

T-14

-15

(request)

Location

Characterization

on SCENE TEN, "SEDUCTION"

"a tiger snake is at the door of his friend's place. he's crying til he throws up in the sink. 'my wife wants me to hit her. she doesn't ask, but she pushes me. she makes me put my hands up and gets this look, the whole eye black and covering—all the air, I wanted to hit her, I wanna take pictures of her in undress. it's not enough sex in my head. the body documented and spread, I am a lucky man,' he cries."

"a tiger snake goes hunting early on a saturday with the guys and he dies in the car. the guns are all in back empty. they call a few people, and they call his wife once he can't get any colder. he's in the window of an ambulance, and the guy's wife has her face to the glass. she's crying, and she's drinking from a tall can. she asks, 'how'd he go?'"

seduction

they're all looking at each other.

"well what *was* it" she asks, "you think I'm gonna interfere with him?"[7] his friend pushes up on the bill of his hat, and stretches his chest forward. buttoned shirt tight to the skin, "maybe you wouldn't be bad to interfere with."[7] he hooks his thumbs on his orange safety vest. he fixes his buckle, his eyes hitting hers, then the buckle.

"I didn't hear nothing."

"can you at least tell me what he last said? that he was maybe thinking of me? we'd just had this fight. I told him I was waiting for him to die with you all, on the corner of a pool table, to the windshield of his truck. low life. dark ride. my own tunnel to love or whatever the metaphor's getting at. whichever is the greater feeling. whatever drove him to the pay phone. he tells me he wishes he had've used that rope I brought, hoping he would really lose it, he should've got lost and gave me something more than kids, this house, what I've always wanted. since I could finally see myself in pictures clicking for him, 'you're good, baby, but you're my tweety bird no more. I miss you. I miss what we had. I'm determined to find it again. some little girl is gonna suck me off tonight.'

"I hung up. I knew then I was gonna pray, and god was gonna do. I wept when I heard the answer. the spirit scrolled the tv guide. listing:

"'3635 VERBENA ROSE CT'

"where the girl begs, and clenches the bed. she puts her hands out behind her, and her wrist bends fingertip to forearm on his hips. she's willing to shoot, just ease into things. she thinks she's supposed to like it, that's how the film was pitched to her, who would ensure anything else, assuming, assuming he came home. he told me it's what we all want. every girl he's fucked with one fixation. I'm at the computer with my legs open, and he's watching like there's a window. like he's a stranger touching himself to someone else's wife. I go to bed. someone gets in the other side. he lives to fish."

the guys are all looking down at their shoes. they're hard against their zippers, but she doesn't know. he tells his wife there was nothing done but a look, but a sadness for the aging of her body, this could've been a dream. god, I don't even consider it settling. god help me, I wanted her.

"when you're over me that's not my real face, baby, I'm anyone you wanna hurt—"

I know, I know.

"he can't leave me, after what he's done to me, who will have me, who's gonna take me now all used up?" the worn straps of her top slide off the top of the cup, folded down over the fullness of her bust.

"I hear you." he pulls down on the inseam, and arranges himself in the waist of his jeans. "she had to have known," he tells anyone but his wife, but this woman, and her hold, her hand right behind the fly, she's gotten down, looked up at him, opened her mouth and licked her lips.

"jeez bess," says the friend. "mike wasn't too talky a guy. this time was like he was paying per word! *three-hour trip*, all he says to me is, 'I bit my tongue.'"

the seduction suite

I was alright for a while, short-horned, and the touch, and the sound. I'm losing my mind. I lie on his chest this time. I see a life with him, beautiful kids, and he's stopped drinking. he says he sees it looking down my shoulder, "if our daughter looked like you, I couldn't help myself. if our daughter looks like you, I won't stop myself. accidents, I promise, everyone's thinking it. when I'm not watching you, I'm watching men look you over and want you. I'll bet you spent a lot of time on your father's keys, yeah, yeah, I'll bet lots of guys keep their keys up there. maybe I ought to start getting used to the pressure in my lap. I'm glad you came over. it was hot to see you so young. you're just now getting—no, no, no, you need to listen to me—it drives me wild hearing these penthouse stories. I oughta record you once for our daughter. all you do is turn me on. all touch and sound just turns me on.

"born just like the wife who won't see me anymore, watching women cut open, born of and for pleasure. smooth on the hand. the head deadening, insensitive."

watching dogs with girls he needs to know the intention. he asks, "could you?"

"could I what?"

he looks at the far end of the couch. there is total despair, crawling along the pillows. loose skin, arms from no one place, dragging, the skin, the neck of a touchy step-grandfather, his wife pleaser stained red by hourly insulin, a sort of cheese made of head flesh, a pig's face, he'd fed to me once. I think my mother was there. she lived there. whichever makes you think kindest of her then? I'm expected to live. total despair is in my house. it watches me get dressed. new tiger, new raptor hunting condos, skate in the house for all I care. spit on his cock, and his hands—

"I might cut my nails," he says, "I don't watch, but I read what he writes and I tell you all here of the colors and the smell—

"I'm sorry, I'm sorry, you've lived so long one last thing then—"

then his voice. burrowed insects in the shore calling me down. decay a thousand white stars with red, round skin. I take my shoes off and I get in the sand. blossom, gore, before the light, beyond faith: desire!

I desire love. I get wet loving you. I used to think you were just drunk but my crying, begging for your cum on me, begging for your sleep, you can't help but smile. you say it's not happening tonight. just the dim ache. a dog as a toy. seamcutter. threadtear. the white undercut, oval seam of the gut, seam of the eye, to water in his thirsty mouth. coat of coats. offal beneath the porch calls more! he wants to watch the dogs together! in his hand, holding himself, his head back, crawl, and satisfy, of its grace unworthy!

unworthy

unworthy

unworthy

yes sir. *when* sir. an audience to have seen the whole thing. a pressure, if no were of thin seals, broken plastic. what he could do to me, after I've done every part of this right, got everything I deserve. I know it's you. just hold my hand for everyone and I'd do anything. all it is, is you're taking down your zipper.

anything, then, then.

JERRY LEE LEWIS' "AND HIS BANNER OVER ME WAS LOVE" (feat. JIMMY ELLIS)

FROM LAST TANGO IN PARIS *(1972)*

"for myra"

MUSIC NO. 00 "AND HIS BANNER OVER ME WAS LOVE"

TUNING: STANDARD

[PAUL rapes JEANNE anally.]

LYRICS:

JERRY:
it's the flash first

JERRY:
then the sound beached at the steps of what it is I do for you // when I'm without my meanness // your even song runs the valley // the rise has big glass faces // light from the lip out // good words this way shot off her cupid's bow // drawn in sand // stone of copper cast fat from the offering's loin // melt up the earth all hard and shiny

GUEST:
gemmed cherry // set stone // be brought to his bed // set ring // of another woman's hand // tell me what you'll do // belly up beneath my keeper // his hand on one side // his hand on the other // raised to be shown and laid down easy

JERRY:
some kind of animal

GUEST:
a stupid animal // he opens my mouth // my tongue swings wild for the coming grace // my tongue writhes right out

of the sheets and falls to bed in fever // oh god // I think I understand this

JERRY:

I want it upright // pedestal // I don't collect // I don't know what suits me

GUEST:

I get in your line and hope for the best // I wish you'd hurt me while you were in my mouth // I wish I'd found the one who'd make the call when I go lame // lead me to the ditch and you aim // tell me go ahead and throw up everything now // and laugh // wipe it down // what are we gonna do out in the grass with no cattle dog // our big nails split and pus without our master // without his violent hand // he bites it out and whistles little funny shit // king of hollywood by the eagles // the mouth wets up my wool

JERRY:

eagles // eagles

GUEST:

I wet up my wool // I have nightmares about my doorway // the dark comes in like a man // he puts his keys in his pocket and he sits me down // it's sick you're scared // twist up what you want // it was never yes but it was never no either // when I look back—

GUEST:

I don't look back

GUEST:

I'm out in the pasture of another man's arms // clear the gate and wire // throw the rope across my tongue and neck // and one wrist up like I'm flexing // how you want me // cuts dark red at the bends of a hot body // of my muscle and my desire // I study the tapes you send with all the glide of thick deep spit // wipe it down after // this time is kinda like I'm in your arms // amur in a great way // in the den of your bright future // coupe of your delight // please violence // yes!

GUEST:
new roads be driven out // frontiersman and bride // and trophy of virility in your doorway // a good dream // I call this loving myself

JERRY:
when you leave // to your left // a switch

GUEST:
through the night light // currant red devoured me // inside // lining the gut // men bring it down and get on top but I must undress myself // how fast I am growing up! // make me useful to the body greater

GUEST:
tell me it was wrong what we did // tell me you were so angry // and I was so willing // the cost of soap is rising // where's your woman?

JERRY:
at the fair // she's holding hands with boys // she's turning up her skirt // the cost is a gate in the grass

GUEST:
I hate myself // I jump on weak knees and collapse into my shoes // how could I get out // no // that hurts me // before the clouds of air-soft sickness // firemen shove around

dirt for survivors // I am alone // I mix glitter in my lotion
// I shine in any light that first time // the next time it's
a blur // the last bears big teeth // salts cars // marrow
frames // I've long been jealous of the taste for strapping
// innovation // excellence // in handling the tight and bare

GUEST:
wow! // he puts the cars right to his mouth and rips and
rips idolatry

GUEST:
wow! // he's coming right at me // how will I say no // that
hurts me // to see killer over there alone

JERRY:
I get the girl dog and I make her lie with him // and the
girls are just as beautiful as their mother // and the boys
are carried off in the mouths of birds // root with seed and
the meat off your arms // an offering:

JERRY:
it's not good enough // a sacrifice:

GUEST:
ten lambs // a hundred lambs he ate skin first // bleating
on my lap // I promise them something new in healing's
place // something for the xbox // the undersides of my
arms are raw and still flexing // the cost of soap paid with
gratitude

JERRY:
happiness is here // open up and receive

GUEST:
pleasured nauseous // the world is soft grass edging you on

GUEST:

birds above ball up and wind down for me // and tell me that I belong // the center by which they find themselves and loved others // thank you // thank you // they take me up against them // the embrace runs me through the shredder // I'm in tatters // my chest shows through big cuts // my hands would do more good // your hands even better

JERRY:

I wouldn't know how to talk if I didn't want anything from you // light steps up to heaven // where I can just ask and be given // I've got to learn to pray

GUEST:

to tread water in his loving body // visions of the surf from the window and magazines thereafter // plastic // with my name and my condition // the end is goodbye and promises of more in months // "I'll see you again" // over beads // banner // I've tried my best // I didn't want to talk that way but it was the cost // and he's losing interest

JERRY:

oh god I can't take it*

----

*liner note: I'm tearing skin over you I'm red over you I ache when I cum I've gotta see a doctor over you you know you fuck like I'm the last man on earth that reminds you of your father you know I've been thinking and what we did I could make you really sick if I wanted if I got sick myself it'd be easy to make you sick too the ache moves through the shaft my balls are drawn up high I'm told this is my body expressing it's virility getting ready to load you up baby I want you to get them both in your mouth and pull down gently work the ache work the ache work the ache

GUEST:

dog in shoes!

GUEST:

dog in coat!

GUEST:

blue sheets // paul // white comforter // a lace skirt // I don't get hungry // who hurts anymore? // paul // looking up at figures // resin lives shown cheap at the bottom // a man came in with his daughter and listened to every word she said // I go outside and I get so sad // I find my worth in pictures // I'm a g cup now // mirrors center me in their image // look!

GUEST:

I walk up the pier // white lace // I hold the hem and you'll do whatever for me // this feather quality to the light // and these expensive cameras // you'll do whatever // if I just lay there // if I just sweat // kill what ails me // you cup your hands around my air and carry it outside to the stoop // animals // skin tight over model plaster // of their own life // and shape do nothing they're dead // I'm dead // thank you for making me feel pretty // I'm the third girl this week // I've got your kid's eyes // paul? // what made you like that? // come on, open up the under

JERRY:

ground // and in the forest you leave all your skin and pain on the grass // on tv // this is real life footage // we show you the dead before anyone else // your friends don't get that kind of *value* // that kind of *bargain* // you'd split at the jaw off his plaster // you'd never get laid // what's there to write about then, huh? // stone altar // you bright // good boys // and your collars

GUEST:

I am beautiful and young // vines of passion flower put my wrists over my head // the one that talks to god turns me on my stomach // tucks my knees up under me // oh god // I think I'm really starting to get this // my hands under my cheek // is a gesture of care // this is a fantasy of mine // I keep back black clouds and fire // from our felicity // he lays down with me // and we look up at all we kept blue // the ash sits in our eyes // I've changed nothing about myself to be happy // it's just cold right now // the fog slumped over the rocks coming to get me // it means something that he cares // I cry in his backseat // I take my clothes off in his backseat // a man I don't know is in the window // I used to jump // I'd feel bad about it but now // you know // 60 men around the couch telling him how to touch me // where to touch me // how hard to touch me // what hurts // feels good to my body

JERRY:

matching looney tunes polos

JERRY:

kachina doll coyote // a little girl tells her dad what to say and he says it // cars are coming // they'll ruin your skin for me // get off the road // get home and get sent my pictures where you're bloody // I wanna hold you // you don't pick up // you don't have the means to pick up right now

GUEST:

have a daughter // put your hand on her leg // how do you wanna breathe when you touch her?

JERRY:

pleasure in the mouth // out

GUEST:

is a public pool in south phoenix // a bike ride at kiwanis // oh god // I feel so guilty // I've killed so many women I've never met // she put my face to the floor I had to do it // she might as well have burned my face in the carpet the way she treated him // I have to defend myself // laws to keep me safe when you come in my fucking house // but I feel guilty // they didn't have to suffer // I took every drop and I wrote to you about how it fell from the body greater // purpose exalted // I feel I could do anything // even love myself // the panel van beside the lake

JERRY:

I've got my gun // you're at the bottom // thigh high in the water // when I look at you it burns down my legs // I take it out of my pocket and I aim // and make you give it up // years later, leathered down // wet temples // the big switch overhand for the governor under

GUEST:

touch hands at a concert // think it means something // I make myself sick with hope // dim your lights then mine // fires rejoice outside the gate // two story signs // itemized loss: // one child and all that time looking // cold out // I wanted in the warmth of your prayers // rings and proposals // I'm outside a trailer // I'm nine and crying

// the spirit perfect was overwhelming // a twin a second behind your words // it drove me to kill with a point // and a talent // and a distinction // between the way my teeth sit in her skin and yours

GUEST: JERRY:
I   [*I*]

GUEST: JERRY:
am going to   [*am going*]

GUEST: JERRY:
hurt   [*to hurt*]

GUEST: JERRY:
you.   [*you.*]

JERRY:
changed // your back rips // spills out all the guilt

JERRY:
I want you for the way you ever carried it a day or two // to get it on my tongue // then eternity // cloud lasting // death in hot weather // no one thinks a thing of us

GUEST:
the cover of the movie // is two hands that wanna touch // a minivan // we sit laps on the way to water

JERRY:
she drinks mickey's and she drives

GUEST:
the satin of our lord makes your banner // angels take a corner each and lift it high // below a dark cast // safe to undress and say I want you // I've never known it not to hurt to say such things // say it back // a textured dream

// psychic readings half off: // he has to stop // he has to see us

JERRY:

the lord split us in two // one our hubris // the other a ford tudor // of our humility // never ask to be whole again // this is a gift // be split again // it's a thready pulse

GUEST:

it's a man on the bus screaming at another // and the fathers and the husbands move their love to the inside seat // I am without // I move myself inside and hope for the best // blood on the door can do

JERRY:

watch the spirit perfect go over us in bright white // the man who killed you has hitchhiked home with it // a broken nose // he left the ford with you // he went up the middle // the road was split the same as us but he longed for oneness // how fast were you going? // I heard it was 80 // I heard your foot slid left of the clutch // speed unmatched became the eve of an ending day // sumac // asters // across his sky // cedar beams // fir rafters // east and love // and love saved // we all drink from the same coke // and eat of his flesh // enriched wheat // dyed syrups cellared for hard times

GUEST:

he sits across two seats to be near me

GUEST:

the lord's got a crush on me // he gets turned on looking in a mirror // we can't go steady, but he touches me anyway // a 12 point in his eyes // death is a reason not to go any further // or it's another gift // an absence of pain while skinned // with my shape and markings // he had no choice // and you've got no choice either // and I sure don't

GUEST:

I get scared and I service him // and I don't remember what's happening to me // but I dream I am beautiful and young and // oh god // it feels— // oh god // I know what I'm doing!

GUEST:

he drives // I'm seeing again all those girls waiting for him to stop // I'd give up my seat to anyone // perdition // skin on skin // welcomes the opening of a car door // rattles the plastic

JERRY:

I'm the rocket engineer // I live to die in a civic // the wall was important work // the house good taste // I put my foot down and I go // I cut my wife because I haven't got the nerve to make something of my own heart

JERRY:

the trailer lets us out to watch violent movies // and watch violent porn // a picture of flamingos taken from the tram // grass and rocks // a lion in it somewhere // he's in your window somewhere you don't see // oh god, I could kill you the same // quiet

JERRY:

the scream fades in // the scream ramps // distort and echo // wait on the sun and burst // shatter my care // a road with no corners // all signs and drives meaningless // unending

GUEST:

through the bottle he lets me stay tonight // the room's breaking up // angels take a flame each // and reach at one another's hand but it never comes down // it speaks to me a gift wept for many nights // possessed // if I'd just put out lust in the baptismal font // smear ash of this quittance in a star over my face // and I'm dying and birthed dying // the sheets are next // immolated in visions of—

GUEST:

and his banner over me was love

JERRY:

and my banner covers the surrey

GUEST:

america goes as far as the eye can see

JERRY:

the rest is in my pocket

GUEST:

can you hear it passing? // can you hear it leaving you?

JERRY:

stop!

GUEST:

I try to look away // and you call after

JERRY:

stop // I'm asleep daddy // I'm asleep jerry!

GUEST:

stop!

JERRY:

when I'm falling asleep I feel you touching me and I know

it's you // daddy // you blame my brother but I know it's
you

GUEST:

can't I sleep? // you're driving me crazy!

GUEST:

can't I put words to it? // can't I move and wake you // it's
what I always wanted

GUEST:

he reeks of it, my care, our—

GUEST:

well

GUEST:

this isn't anything is it.

THE DICK CAVETT SHOW
(ABC, 1973)

TONIGHT:

clip from "last tango in paris"

ALT TEXT:

PAUL SHOWS UP IN A CYCLING SHIRT AND MATCHING SHORTS, IN THE SENSE THAT THEY LOOKED ALRIGHT TOGETHER, HE'S RESPONED TO THE CLASSIFIED, IN THE SENSE THAT THIS IS A DISCOVERY OF THE UNMAPPED, OR THE MAPPED AND LIED ABOUT, IN THE SENSE THAT THIS CAN'T BE, AND HE CAN'T SEEM TO READ THE SITUATION, IT'S NOT NO, IT'S WELL, NOW WHAT? IS THIS ALRIGHT?

MARLON BRANDO AS PAUL IN *last tango in paris*:

>> TELL ME ABOUT YOUR FATHER

PART ONE:

ALT TEXT:

SHE CLIMBS THE BLACK LEATHER MOUNT.

>> YOU'RE NOTHING LIKE MY FATHER. YOU'RE NOTHING LIKE MY DAD.

MY DAD WOULDN'T LOOK AT ME FOR DAYS. MY BROTHER NEVER EXISTED, BUT I USED TO. THE GRADES, AND THE AWARDS. ACHIEVEMENT WIDENED THE DISTANCE. I GOT STUPID AND IT DID NOTHING EITHER. ONE DAY, I WEAR THESE SHORTS.

HE TELLS ME, IN FRONT OF EVERYONE— EVERYONE WAS OVER FOR A HOLIDAY— COME SIT ON MY LAP. OUR COUCH WAS LOW FROM WEAR, AND YOU COULD REALLY LEAN INTO IT. HE SAT ALL THE WAY IN, AND SET HIS HAND ON MY BACK. IT RODE ME DOWN TO THE TOP OF MY ASS, AND IT LINGERED. I FELT LIKE—

IT FELT LIKE WHEN I WATCHED SEX ON TV.

HE ALWAYS INSISTED I KNEW WHAT I WAS DOING. I KNEW ALL ABOUT SEX, I WAS TALKING SHOP. I WAS A KID. I WAS

HUMILIATED. BUT EVERYONE WAS WATCHING, SO HOW BAD COULD IT HAVE BEEN?

>> *I DON'T KNOW. YOU'RE PRETTY BRUISED UP. I DON'T KNOW WHAT TO TELL YOU.*

Q: YEAH, BUT THAT'S NOT ACTING[8]

A: WHEN YOU'RE FRIGHTENED AND NERVOUS IN THIS CHAIR, OR YOU'RE VERY ANGRY, AND YOU KNOW THAT IS NOT WHAT IS NECESSARY... THAT CANNOT BE SHOWN NOW. YOU'RE A HIGHLY CONTROLLED PERSON. [9]

Q: WHAT I MEAN IS... YOU SAY THAT THAT'S ACTING, I DO NOT. I AM MOTIVATED. DO THAT SAME PERFORMANCE BEFORE A CAMERA AND DO IT AGAIN AND AGAIN, I CAN'T. YOU SEEM TO DO IT BETTER THAN ALMOST ANYBODY.

A: NO, THAT ISN'T TRUE.

A: I thought I'd have more control. I've turned down happiness in several states of undress, spread for me, I was certain I could stop myself. walk him down in a corner. this fantasy I don't dream ends. all action upfront, and constant. molding of the home. breaking in his bed to give to my brother. breaking my dresser because it frustrated him as a man. looking down one shelf to the next, it says, "I want a rich son. I want a perfect son, I wanna be adored, I must, I must.

"I didn't mean anything by it."

I know you didn't. you wanted me to grow up. to get sick of denying myself the pasture of my own skin. the soft clover of my needs met, and wholly satisfied.

Q: LET'S GO TO A CLIP FROM AN EARLIER WORK, *lot's daughters lot's daughters brought out to you, and you may do to them as you wish.*

EDMUND:

I've got so much anger in me. I look at it all on a table, what's been done to me, it's not so bad. it's no worse than any other kid gets it. but if I were a dog, and you were my neighbor, looking over your fence, there would be calls. there would be some sort of shame on his part, if only because you knew. who wants to get caught standing too close to their dog? who wants to be the guy looking down their dog's shirt? dogs don't ask for it like women. he felt me up in a room full of family. his girlfriend was the only one who said anything. I'm so whipped. I'm so sick that I start the spin. I told her it was fine and then, I guess I went to bed. it's black after for months. I've lost a lot of time. the way I tell it, I was born seven, my poor mother. he didn't like black chicks much, he just got something out of pressing them hardest, my poor mother. she loved a really sick guy. she thought I was going to kill my brother. she said she was gonna send me away. she said I'd get this look, and no one meant anything to me. I love you all. it's like one big party for everyone you know and you just can't get buzzed. I'd have done anything to—I've got control. I used to think sleeping was like death. I was scared to sleep as a kid. suddenly it's all I can do. that's control. that's how you keep the people you love safe. you die a little all the time. my father would stay up for days. I just wanted him to love me like the other kids were loved, not the women. everyone always told me I was beautiful like a woman. I wanted to be a little boy, more than anything, I'd have hurt anyone. there. I've got to be honest. the way he'd watch me eat. my mother loved me, but she was out of her depth. if she had've just said it, owned her shame about me, I would've—who knows. I was ten, and I had to change a lightbulb. I'm in the dark, and I stick my hand in the socket. the way it washed over me. I didn't understand what was happening. I wasn't a smart child. I just didn't want it to happen again. I go to my mom, I tell her, "I tried to change it myself, but it hurt me."

"so what," she says, "you want me to get shocked?" who knows that anything would've changed. I wish her well. I wish her a kid who marries.

Q: BUT IF YOU HAD TO TAKE THE LINE 'LEONARD, THAT'S TERRIFIC,' SIX TIMES AND GET SOMETHING DEEPER—TIME AFTER TIME—THAT TAKES AN ACTOR.

A: THE DIALOGUE CHANGES ALL THE TIME.

A: my mother still loves him. she says she can't help but to, can't I see it? can't I feel it? deserve it. look just like him. no, no, you drink like him, but he doesn't care what a hummingbird sounds like. smoking oil. wet fingers, and you're what's beneath me, at the foot of the oven, and we're all over at a friend's place. I never lost a thing. I didn't even flinch anymore. I was gonna be the man. she says congratulations. I grip the chair. I look like I might hit her. a second greater welcome for my success. my father's portrait: my father's hands around the chair's arms like he might shoot. whoever you are, you know, it's like a tomb, and everything I love gets buried with me because I didn't love it right.

he had this fantasy. the desire to see it made flesh, and begging, was blinding. the almighty accelerant. the speedometer and it's direct line to one jesus h. christ in heaven. he sits up out of the driver's seat. he's on the wheel like it's storming, and the asphalt is gonna wave up and break us in half. the kids in back going away, sinking. me and him, the adults upfront.

"for you, for all the sexy little things like you, I'll never be broken," he says. "a man's got a right to make himself happy."

"the deer overrun the place otherwise," I say, just

when I'm supposed to. it was my will to eat the grass to nothing. I've got no sense.

"look at what you do. when you're out for yourself, look how your mother suffers," he says. I know what I did. I understand that I don't get what's so bad. I understand I lack moral tenacity.

"I forgive you!" he says. "puberty is changing for everyone."

PART TWO:

ALT TEXT:

HE PUTS ALL HIS WEIGHT ON HER OPEN LEGS.

>> *I REMEMBERED I GOT SO HOT TYRING TO KEEP COVERED WHILE I SLEPT. 18 YEARS, I ALMOST ALWAYS HAD MY OWN BED AT MY MOM'S. MY DAD NEVER EVER BOUGHT ME ONE, ONCE. HIS GIRLFRIEND GAVE ME THE ONLY ONE I'D HAD OVER THERE. THEY BROKE UP, AND SHE TOOK BACK THE BED, AND HIS MOTHER MOVED BACK IN, AND I GOT MOVED DOWN TO THE COUCH.*

HE KEPT THE HOUSE HOT. IT WAS A CORDUROY COUCH, AND I RUN HOT. YOU CAN TELL. EVERYONE ALWAYS SAYS THAT, THAT I'M TOO WARM, AND I'VE GOT TO GET AWAY FROM THEM. IT HAD BECOME INTOLERABLE. I WOULD WEAR AS LITTLE AS I COULD AND TRY TO BEAT EVERYONE WAKING UP. HE WAS ALWAYS THERE WHEN I'D OPEN MY EYES. AND EVERYONE WAS TALKING. I JUST HAD TO LAY THERE. HE WOULDN'T GO UPSTAIRS. EVERYONE ELSE TAKES THE HINT, OR

FINDS SOME BUSINESS, AND HE'S SITTING AT THE OTHER END OF THE COUCH, TALKING TO ME. AND THERE I WAS, HUMILIATED AGAIN. HE USED TO JOKE ABOUT HOW HIS DAD TOOK HIS DOOR OFF HIS ROOM. "THIS WILL CUT DOWN ON YOUR 'PLAY TIME.'" I HEARD THAT STORY A THOUSAND TIMES AND THOUGHT, POOR GUY. I TOLD THIS STORY ONCE, AND THEY FELT SO BAD FOR ME. IT WAS EMBARASSING.

I DIDN'T LIKE WHAT THEY HAD TO SAY ABOUT MY DAD THEN. I'D DRAW UP THIS COMFORTER WITH THESE CIGARETTE BURNS. I DIDN'T KNOW WHAT THEY WERE AT THE TIME. I DIDN'T LOOK TOO HARD INTO STUFF, MY DAD DIDN'T LIKE FOR ME TO DO THAT. NEITHER OF US SMOKED. I DON'T KNOW WHERE IT CAME FROM. I'D DRAW IT TIGHT AROUND MY NECK AND COOK, UNTIL I JUST COULDN'T TAKE ANYMORE.

PAUL STRUGGLES TO MAINTAIN AN ERECTION, BETRAYING THE EXCITEMENT, BECOMING FRUSTRATION ON HIS FACE. HE LOOKS DOWN AT A KNOTTED HAND. AN OVERUSED HAND IN THE TRASH.

>> *IS THAT MINE?*

>> *YOU CAN HAVE IT BACK IF YOU WANT.*

>> *WOULD YOU LOOK AT THAT.*

>> *MY FATHER'S CALLING. DO YOU WANT ME TO ANSWER?*

>> *I DON'T KNOW. I'LL KNOW WHEN YOU CUM. I'LL FEEL IT.*

>> *TAKE IT.*

>> *OKAY, SURE!*

>> *DON'T TALK SO MUCH.*

>> *SURE THING!*

Q: ARE YOU TELLING ME I CAN PLAY ANY ROLE YOU CAN AS GOOD AS YOU?

A: I DON'T THINK I COULD PLAY THE ROLE YOU PLAY NOW.

A: I laid my head to the glass, and closed my eyes a second.

he says "blessings every day become pigeons." he pulls back and forth on the wheel. I'm hitting my head on the window playing sleep. I'm hitting my head, thinking he'll get bored of me. I'm really getting height on the wind up. I'm practically upright. I wake up, about to hurt myself. "I thought you were asleep."

I had a regular partner in sex around 25, and when we were together, it was hard to picture either of us leaving to a steady job. we were so empty, and so pathetic. so afraid to tell the other that this is too much, to be soft for the other. I remember we caused each other great pain. I felt accomplished after every lay, the way people lift weights, and run far, the farthest they've ever gone. the pride washing them. the pride making their eyes dark and round, mostly. the afternoon cuts in the window, in a line from my mouth to his genitals.

the afternoon cuts in the windshield. I'm in the passenger seat, and my father's just told me my eyes look just like a woman's. they're—his hand's on my knee—they're, oh, just take the complement. just forget it. you are just an unsatisfactory partner. you get yourself ready then, and I'll just hit my mark. intimacy is held in place and told to relax like anyone else.

Q: I'D LIKE TO SHOW ANOTHER CLIP FROM lot's daughters.

EDMUND:

she wanted me to start carrying some sort of protection. she thinks it's 'cause I'm proud I don't, when really I'm just angry. I've got these fantasies where I beat myself to death. I leave my face unconscionable. I've got others where I'm being pressed, I get you off me, and I get on you. I've got the right of way. I cry. I do what I'm supposed to. "I'd never kill anyone, I can't fathom the guilt, but his face, god, my hands." you look at my back here and tell me you've got a chance. you look at that picture and tell me I'm gonna be okay. I begged to wear my brother's coat. it was green, with military stars, and varsity numbers. while we were out having fun, my dad and me, I didn't have a brother. my dad always insisted on having fun. my dad always insisted there was only so much fun to go around. and when he finally threw my brother out, he had plenty. I guess that's what I don't get, why it's so bad for me to enjoy myself. I played sports, and went to sleepovers. I waited for childhood to finally take hold. they all seemed so young now. they really couldn't take much. I realized I had this extreme quality to me. I either want "it"—and you could only ever be "it" back then—I either want "it" or I don't. I'd check out psych books from the library. I spent hours flipping through symptoms because I believed that if I could name it, well, I'm getting somewhere. I'd know who to talk to. everything always came back dire. I thought I was being dramatic. "I'm young," I thought. no one's diagnosing under 18. I heard they are now. I wonder if I

was close. I'm young! what kid thinks that? I was scared
all the time. I believed that when you watched ghosts on
tv, the home would generate these images. oh, between
him, and the movies—and I didn't have a room by then,
I was on the couch. I'd fall asleep once the backyard went
purple. before it got a good healthy color. all day we get
bruised up, and at night it's like god's healing. bruises
don't always heal, did you know that? I've got a scar right
above my knee. I can't believe how hard I was hitting. part
of what I did here was learn to stop doing that. they've
got me in this therapy for the traumatized. I don't ever
want to be myself again. I've got no control then. I've
got to keep this distance. it's you, the door, then me. the
therapy is to get me to open the door, but you can hear
me. I think it's like shaving. I think it's good hygiene to
keep the distance.

Q: I JUST FEEL LIKE ALL MY CLOTHES HAVE BEEN TAKEN OFF. LET'S SEE IF YOU'RE ANY GOOD AT IT. ALL YOU DO IS LOOK UP. HAVE FUN WITH IT.

A: NO, I WON'T DO IT.

A: I got in my father's car. we're talking about the oscars. some actor. it didn't matter. I was talking back. it was a matter of respect that he floor it.

"what do you deserve?" he's in and out of our lane and I couldn't walk from there. out past the reservation, near the highway and cattle, "you don't deserve a thing." gila river. we'd just been to visit family out there. he's all over the road, and I gotta take a deep breath and ask myself what cousin charlie's place looks like. I remember: my father and I played catch in a green expanse. there were other boys, and I'd outperformed them, and everyone made a point of telling him congratulations, you oughta be proud, and he was, and maybe a little flattered, and maybe looking at me a little too long.

I got in my father's car, and he tells me if he were still a young man, it'd really hurt. what's been shown is discipline. "can you imagine how I've been hurt? I do all this to you and oh, I feel empty," he says, "you don't move me anymore," he says, "you really look upset. and this world is of my flesh, I think," he says, "I think my kid died sometime in the second grade, and you came out of the pool wet and slight, and not knowing any better, gripping your chair like a gun. acting strangely for the sake of my life. what a kid, to circle the wagons like that. we make a way for what matters."

as for my life, I'm not worried I don't know how to make anything. houses are bought, and so is love, and I do alright for myself.

you know, I never saw charlie again.

PART THREE:

ALT TEXT:

HE DUMPS THE PURSE. HE GETS ALL THE LIPGLOSS AND LINES THEM UP BY SIZE. HE'S GOING TO INSERT THEM INTO HER—BOTH WAYS TO SEE WHAT HE LIKES. MAYBE SHE WEARS IT AFTER?

>> PAUL, HAVE YOU FELT IT?

>> NO

>> I'VE BEEN TRYING. IT'S BEEN DONE.

>> ALRIGHT.

>> IF IT'S BEEN DONE, WE OUGHT TO STOP.

>> I JUST DIDN'T FEEL IT.

>> THAT'S ALRIGHT. YOU WERE WONDERFUL.

>> I'VE BEEN WITH WOMEN BEFORE, YOU KNOW, YOU'RE NO PUZZLE.

>> I'M TELLING YOU, WHATEVER YOU WANTED TO DO TO ME TONIGHT, IT'S BEEN DONE.

>> WOULDN'T I KNOW IT?

>> YES.

>> WHEN IT HAPPENS?

>> YES, PAUL.

>> IT HASN'T HAPPENED YET.

>> *I UNDERSTAND. MY DAD COULD NEVER MAKE A CALL, HE WAS WISHY-WASHY.*

>> *ALRIGHT.*

>> *YOU'LL TELL ME WHEN YOU'VE GOT WHAT YOU WANTED. YOU COMMUNICATE. I LIKE THAT ABOUT YOU. HAVE YOU FELT IT YET?*

>> *I DON'T KNOW WHAT I WANT.*

>> *I LOVE THE WAY YOU TALK.*

>> *I'M TIRED.*

>> *LAY BACK THEN.*

>> *I DON'T KNOW.*

>> *YOU DON'T WANT ME?*

>> *YOU'RE VERY PRETTY. THIS IS VERY GOOD FOR ME. I DON'T KNOW WHAT I'M SAYING.*

>> *WORK ME OVER. I'M ASKING YOU TO.*

>> *I ALWAYS FEEL BETTER AFTER I HURT SOMEONE.*

>> *I FEEL GOOD ABOUT YOU TOO.*

Q: WELL, IF I LOOK AT THEM AND SAY NOTHING, THE SHOW BECOMES SO QUIET.

A: YOU GET A FACE FOR IT AND YOU DO IT DAY AFTER DAY AFTER DAY.

A: my mother begs me to forgive him. I let go of the chair. it's hard not to drink. it's hard to really love anyone, knowing how they think. when god sends down the angels to lot, and the men start to circle, they say, "I know I am never in harm under His light, I know I am righteous," whispering to one another, "we are His children, and we were sent down perfumed.

"what was I supposed to let happen?"

"I don't know," lot says. "I'd know when it was done."

Q: LET'S GET ANOTHER CLIP FROM lot's daughters.

EDMUND:

the night it all got away from me, my father had this look. I
read a lot about sad kids, and unwell men. they talk about
the crying they both do, you know, the shame. he always
smiled. he always had a good time. I just let him get it
over with. he was having fun, and things had been so hard
before. that's how we got here. this was his home by the
rites of nature. I'd smile too. he liked it better that way. he
got angry when he went through the trouble of hurting
me and didn't like it. I don't think of myself as a victim.
it's hard to admit a complete lack of control. he liked to
laugh, so I made him laugh. I gained weight, lost weight,
stopped showering. he was relentless in his pursuit of the
joy and the laughter he thought he deserved. I suppose I
am too. he couldn't hurt me anymore, he was in no shape
to fight anymore, but I just couldn't help myself. I'm just
a happy guy. I'm an inquisitive guy, and I take note of
wires and tubing. it's always important when you see it.
you oughta start seeing it too. the day it got away from
me, at the hospital, he wanted me to make him smile.
he demanded it, after giving so much. private school,
college apartments, club sports, they cost. I'd give him
all the money back if he'd wait a minute. I never wanna
hear about the money again. these cords around the leg
of my chair. "I'd never kill anyone, I can't fathom the
guilt," but this desire, too, is blinding. it's like I'll never
eat again. it's like my smile's gone for good under these
wires, and tubing, and cords. it's always the guys who
really throw their size around that get stuck on youth.

people get arrested, I realized, because they never settled in the fear. they know it's this posturing, what their father does to them. I was scared to death of my father. until he had his accident, I knew he'd do whatever he wanted. he had up until that point. sometimes I remember his lap. he'd call me over. I remember just how whatever it was felt on my backside. I ask every man I meet where he keeps his keys. there's no real alignment in where they go from pervert to honest, but the consensus was: whichever side I wasn't on. I'd never considered my comfort! he never asked my brothers over. they didn't have the build. he always said we'd make beautiful kids, if I weren't his kid. I'm tense with kids. I don't wanna be around them. it's nothing about them. I don't like being around dogs either. too much trust in me, and faith in me. I'm not some pervert, but they wouldn't really know that. I didn't know who was a pervert, anyway! I hope it's the same. I hope I'm not just stupid. the nurse talks to me like I'm his wife. he's flattered. he smiles. I think it's in us all to hurt a child someway.

Q: NO, IT ISN'T!

A: WE COULDN'T SURVIVE A SECOND IF WE DIDN'T LEARN TO ACT. TO SAVE OUR LIVES, ACTUALLY, EVERY DAY.

A: "I wanna see what you bought from the mall. I wanna hold it myself." my uncle is in the passenger seat. this is very upsetting for him. my father holds out the little shorts to him, and when he doesn't receive, he holds it to me. "what is this?" stroking, "what is this?"

"do you want me to return it?"

"no, no." back in the bag. out on the body, right away, and show me. I come down and I show the family what a slut I am. I acted, for my uncle, and my father. for me, and the gifts I'd keep, like I didn't know what was happening to me.

they're telling me he's been in an accident, oh man.

he might not make it. oh man.

it's easy as that?

I didn't miss my shift. work was nothing. I slept like nothing.

today? he's fighting! yeah, good for him. I've got work tonight.

today? he flipped his hand!

yeah, yeah, I'm sweating.

I'm scared I'm 12 again.

NEXT UP (A RETROSPECTIVE):

clip from "years from now you'll be glad you did this"

ALT TEXT:

A YOUNG WOMAN PREPARES HERSELF FOR YOU. IT'S IMPORTANT SHE HAVE A GOOD TIME. WESTERN PLEASURE WILL MAKE SURE YOU DO.

>> *I'M SORTA LIKE A STARLING WHEN I TALK, AND WHEN I LIVE HERE, I'M REALLY HURTING ALL THOSE OTHER BIRDS.*

IT'S IMMORAL TO JUST WATCH!

YOU HAVE TO DO SOMETHING!

MONTGOMERY CLIFT AS WESTERN PLEASURE IN years from now you'll be glad you did this:

blessed waist of this land, copper buckle of this sun belt, homesteader, baby, heaven's in your company. I'm writing songs to get in. I'm talking what's meant to be. it's better than skin. the flesh is a dream. your wife but filthy. your home but fox, and perfumed, and ending and leaving with passing arousal. home on the rip, painted horses in the rush. you dream me, and above, and full of leather, licking up salt.

and above, making love as coats. the moon gives down deliverance, purpose as gripped skin. as eternal as it matters. He fashions something to cover his hands. setter in the rush, and I kill what He has eyes for. He says the rip's filled out, she's a real-life lady.

it crawls, it makes red dirt of these pale, little coasts, and they cry mercy, mercy, I'm your kid, water, the girls in it, have the bleed coming.

death is good of me, and death is kind of Him. I am a man with something sharp. I am perfect silk, covet freely. I live in His image, and I'm grateful for its blessings, and I'm sick all the time. I'm not eating like I should. I'm already dead! this is the bolt, and the bleed, or maybe here is under the bright light, and you are the skinner, or you are with the skinner, but I know you're not mourning. it was a good life on your land, and I am grateful, and I am sick.

on another, on something lighter, I do believe you care. I do think I love you. it's lust all the way, lust for sure. it's the sun halved. loosened belt when you say alright, yes,

yes

yes

yes, I would, and I will, and I want to. get to the edge and look down. the water moves unnatural. the water's stiff just watching. if you're so kind, and you're so good, you'll close your hand to me.

that's very flattering, the way you're slow about it.

the moon is peeling. I see things. I cover myself in the
word. I wet it down sheer for tourists. they check my
mouth for the unclean spirit, my destiny on my tongue,
o, it's in me, o, isn't it delicious!

I close my eyes, and it's something like you're there.
something like I'm praying, and you, Lord, with you—
I've never felt so helpless.

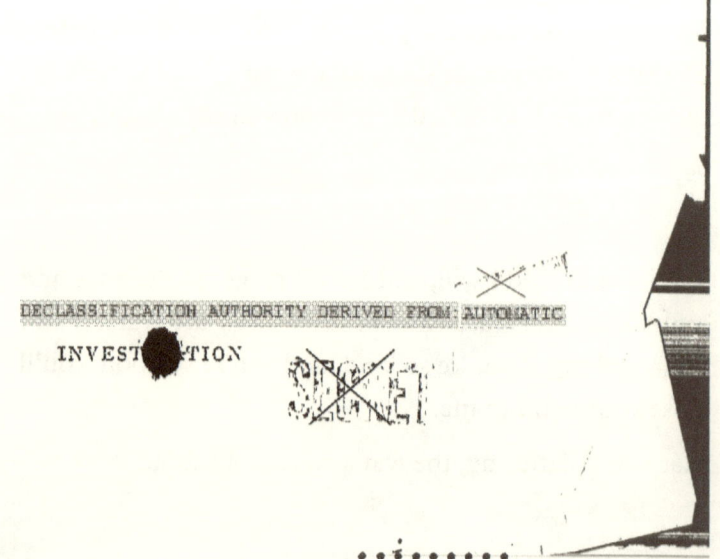

PART FOUR:

ALT TEXT:

PAUL LOOKS DOWN HIMSELF, AND UP AT GOD, AND SEEKS CHARITY OF HIS WILL. THE ROOM KEEPS THE HEAT OF THE SUN, GREAT BE HIS KINDNESS, BUT THE LIGHT IS INTOLERABLE.

>> PLEASE FINISH.

>> I MUST.

>> PLEASE FINISH.

Q: YOU INVITE FRANKNESS. IT BUGS ME THAT OVER THE YEARS YOU'VE ACTED SO LITTLE.

A: IS IT GETTING DULL? THAT'S YOUR JOB. I DON'T TALK ABOUT MOVIES.

A: once he hit his head, he wasn't smooth about asking anymore, you know, "touch me, touch me. I wanna feel something," you know, just take a look.

I'd look at all the cords and think of—

I wouldn't think a thing.

I believe god has left me exactly where he meant to. and I am meant to exact my will and purpose, in his image, with his forgiveness predestined. you as intimacy, and I as the hand, and our image, together, the lips and teeth of god, eating, eating, eating, and full.

my animal life spent pure, hunting my shepherd's lot as he wills it.

Q: ONE LAST CLIP FROM *lot's daughters lot's daughters brought out to you, and you may do to them as you wish.*

EDMUND:

people never considered the pain of it all. "you know, I would fight." "I would fight him off." "I would call the police." "I would run away from home." "I would tell my mother." the pain is like a big, flat hand in the middle of your back. all the air out of your balloon, and the batteries knocked out of your little rc truck. everything becomes terrible, stays terrible in your memory, in your life forward when you see that light, touching yourself, you lay down against carpet and you feel sick. the pain of it all. the pain of medicine, and the pain of getting worse, and worse, "you let it happen." and I guess these people I've hurt let it happen too. you all living must be so brave, and so joyous.

we were out of town for a basketball game. the whole thing was off from the start. my brother was sick, that was one. we'd left in the middle of the night, that was two. we'd left with my coach, who was a cousin of ours, and his kid, that was three. it was always me, and him, and my brother. I thought, since my brother was ill, I was gonna get my own bed. I'd never had my own bed before on vacation. not that this was vacation, I was there to play. I had to be up early the next morning. we check in late. my father's at the desk. my father, he comes over and says "the room's not ready."

when will it be ready?

he takes me upstairs. is the room ready? he won't talk to me. there's only two beds. where am I gonna sleep?

nothing. and I think, oh, he's got me. I walked right into this one. I'd been outfoxed. I couldn't shut my eyes. he slept with his back to me, and I listened all night for him to turn. I stayed up all night watching tv. I played a horrible game the next day, you know, knowing I'd be back in the same place that night. he was angry I was scared in front of his people. that I couldn't turn it off. that I wasn't sitting there drooling for it. he taught me that mountain cats and boars don't let their quarry go because it was so nice, and so compliant. predators have no mercy. getting older is the shed of inhibitions, and the coming of your turn. some push the responsibility of it all. idealists, maybe. I've never seen anyone take responsibility, anyway. I just thought I was the ugliest kid. I was a dirty kid, and everyone knew I touched myself every chance I got, and that I fucking liked it. that was why he was hurting me. that's why my mother knew I was the problem. she was ready to send me wherever would take me, and cut her losses on her fantasy of her oldest boy. my father's got no give. I was the ugliest kid. all I thought about was dying, how it had to happen quick, soon, now. how scared I was for the end, inevitable. I go back in the hospital another hour. I go home and pray. I just need it fixed. my poor mother. I killed him because I wanted to. that's the only reason anyone does it. my mother, she helped me move out of his place, and she didn't know a thing. I left his body right in the bed. I don't care what happens next. I've got no control.

I've got control. it's just it's got nothing to do with you. as I've sat here with you, and begun to be understood by you, I've become squeamish. that's what I'd say being a person is. if I were speaking to my father's dog, I'd say it's skin, and it's nails, and genitals without comfort. with no hope for comfort. as I've sat here with you, I've remembered another story. one last story and I'll stop feeling bad for myself.

I went to a school with no fences. no, we kept the one facing the road, but behind us were fields and canals. arizona doesn't keep much grass. the soft dirt stayed cold longer. our field was trampled, and the dirt was pressed to sedimentary rock. the lower field was some man's, and he treated it well, and let us in from time to time. we'd be inside reading about spider burrows, and we could go out and stick our fingers in their relief. we could wish it for ourselves, eight legs and quiet, and some way to defend ourselves. the sky clear, the air hot, with its hands all over. I remember there was this big dust devil and we all ran toward it, us kids. and as a kid, you know, you've got no real sense of size. everything's more than or less. I have a good sense for less, like all men with my sort of—my kind of issues. the ways in which I'm a danger. and we got them all the time, the dust devils. they were mundane. to see one so dark with—who knows what, that's the draw! the attraction's what if I fly? and the neurotic behaviors are a rock in your head. a rock in my head? no, no, we turn back. one kid stands in it. he says, I won't run, I will stand in my conviction. and the rock in the head leaves this frankenstein kinda scar all the way around his head.

and he says "I welcome you and I love you." my teacher sent him to the office often, and I went to one of those schools where the principal could hit the kids if we were bad enough. if he felt we were bad enough. "I will stand in my conviction," whatever this was. that we shouldn't have to be here. my parents always told me this principal could never touch me. but I'd been sent to the office over a book report, and he said I was a good kid, and I was gonna get this thing done. he said you wanna know how I'll do you? I saw the paddle. I saw what that boy took, and no one felt any guilt about giving. he brought it from behind his desk and put it flat over both hands, height in the air wavering with density, weighty with dream force, perpetual, perpetual force.

I remembered the boy coming back to our trailer, the trailer we had class in, breathless and crying, but only in the eyes. he tightens up and he's a man at his desk. the principal puts it back, the paddle. he sends me back to the trailer. I don't remember if I cried. I hadn't been hit, so I hope not. I hope I was a man like my friend. my friend! I've never said it that way. he was my friend. I was an odd child, I didn't have many. I don't remember if I told my parents, looking back, that the principal had shown me his dream force. how he'd do me. both arms fit in his hand up to the elbow. his perpetual force quarters a kid. they could've been in a lot of trouble! it could've been nothing at all. really saying all this aloud stirs the heart. I'm realizing some sort of love for that boy, as a boy myself. yes, I loved that boy, blond, and blue-eyed, and not much taller than me. not much bigger than me. he swore he was going easy. he let me wrestle, and showboat. he let me because of some sort of similar affection, I hope. I loved him, I hope he loved me back. beautiful boy, brave boy, praying amongst us like he hadn't come from god's gate already. jesus' gate, more delicate. and the kind of love a stretched collar from wrestling in the dirt under the basketball hoop, and a childish lust for parts that hadn't grown in yet. the extreme desire to stand with one another in line, uniformed, facing forward, and I look over his buzzed head, the tall bushes of green exaggerations, bougainvillea petals to the right of his broadening shoulder, and I want to remember it forever as all I needed.

they kept him there long after I left, but I'd already folded. I did the report. my father helped me substantially with the physical art project that my teacher required: a papier mâché figure of a little boy's head with no mouth, and a cat's black eyes, the skull sloping, shaped like an underfilled balloon, with a harsh hairline. he was proud. my teacher, she found it very strange, and my report good enough. I move schools the next year. I don't think about him again until today, with you, when everything's gone to shit.

I come home the night it's poor him. I'm a fucking wreck coming through the doorway. I asked him—I told him, I've always wondered what it was like to do that to me. to feel me up like I'm some woman, you know? it was like he knocked my drink over, and I caught half of it. you know, it's kinda warmer than it was. than you remember. but there's something, and that's good, it really is good enough. we could've put it behind us. he just kept knocking it over. the last of it feels like spit. it's so hot, you don't even want it, but you're scared to let yourself go to waste. and then, all of a sudden, you have nothing left. you start flinching, and you don't take gifts anymore. you're standing up for yourself! it feels like standing on the sun. it feels like a scouring clean, and the thirst. you've got no money, you're a kid. you have no idea what you've done, or how to fix it. you'd do anything for so little. money's no object, you're a kid! nothing really costs that much, just time, and skin, and you've plenty. you look back at those baseball cards, and that's when you realize you had a grip of cash. you realize you paid too high. the whole thing's a lemon.

anyway, to make a long story short, he offers you another can, you take another can. it's nothing complicated.

in short, I ask him how good I must feel. he says, "oh, I suppose you're gonna wanna sit up all night and talk now."

shit.

I looked at him, I said, "no."

I said, "goodnight."[10]

Q: THANK YOU, MARLON!
A: THANK YOU!

1974 NATIONAL SOCIETY OF FILM CRITICS AWARDS

acceptance of "BEST ACTOR"

"now you have to look" he said!
and you clap for me.

I remember I was watching tv. I was sitting there watching steve wilkos, and steve stands over, he asks, "how many times is molestation?" the man grips his chair, getting lower and lower. the channel switched over from the fox affiliate to the network, out to fort lauderdale and they showed me this guy so torn up at the airport you couldn't tell face up from down. there was a shooting at the airport, and they couldn't tell me who this man was. the gun ate his face, and his wallet, and his teeth. the gun cut his hands off.

"it had square eyes, and I could see the paper behind them once he started killing. and his head was on the shoulders of a horse, and he only needed two legs so he'd cut off the other two, and made a tail of his dragging back, wagging. he was so happy to eat. I don't know how I missed the guy." each return to him, white flash over him, covers horror with digital slacks and shoes darker and darker and the socks, jesus, it's a yellow suit, "he's just a business man!" over the pa system. "I'm sorry, I'm sorry, he's just going to work!"

"commutes do awful things to us," I say. I turn over to dexter on cbs.

it's really not up to me, but I do very well for myself.

being as sick as I am, I've seen the gun. it told me I already know who deserves to die. it was making eyes for the man pissing at the train stop. "I'm in love," it says, "he just knows we deserve it." the grass just across the street idle at night, and he can't be bothered, and it reeks. I hate to be touched. I hate to see his cock. he doesn't know what it is does to me. he has no right. "well, I know something about him," it says, "I know just how he comes apart." I sweat in my room, screaming from good health, the both of us, god, help me, it turns me on. "we ought to piss too," it says. no one's ever let me see them soft before. *reward enough!*

I get a check in the mail to live another two weeks. this is good work, to be a dog tearing you with another. this second dog, circumstance. this place, where I can't control myself. we think we're so big, like dogs can't walk on two feet. a soul like anyone's overwhelmed by desire of cessation, to not need for a minute. to not eat in eating. in letting you fuck me, after a while, it's happened, you know, I've seen plates put back together in tubs of milk, but I don't believe it, you know. he didn't finish in me. he wasn't in me at all. he couldn't move from the neck down, and the nurse has got a catheter. a *foley* catheter.

and you laugh for me.

and the nurse says "someone has *got* to *learn* to *use this!*"

and he tells me "now you have to look."

146   sasha hawkins

he couldn't feel me up anymore, so I'd have to hold myself on his hands, you know, he really wasn't such a bad guy when you think about what sluts little girls can be. they wanna watch the movie over and over on your lap. it's in you to start the tape. he would tell me everything that's in him is in you, and you're either scared or you're smart when it gets out all over the floor, and crawling the train to me, getting me wet, the door opened, the fire poured out

> whatever my eyes desired I did not keep from them. I did not withhold my heart from any pleasure, for my heart rejoiced in all my labor; and this was my reward from all my labor[11]

I'm gonna get out of here and take from somebody else, yada, yada. I heard it said to music that there's nothing under the sun. alone with the gun, it told me "you better get going, don't let me keep you."

I maced that man and I talked with him awhile. "now you have to look" I said. and you clap for me.

she took his head and she made many holes, and covered him in thick plastic. she kills to make herself look good in his fine house, and his von dutch hats. she looks for round ends on long objects, fucking herself innate like other kids, *well!*

sometime later I've just been raped by a beautiful man. he walks me to the door and I tell him thank you, and he tells me "oh, this is just life and everyone's living it." I don't have to explain it to you.

you've seen it all. you know just how I operate, waiting until a guy can't defend himself. you already killed him, and you'll do anything to kill him in us. he'd want you to get away with this, that's what's so sad. he died loving you like you were the perfect woman, when all you wanted was to be was his son. low dreams. shortsighted day trades. throw yourself from the window.

from the brick sill, I see him often, looking out at you all, listening, I fear he'll answer. he'll pull up my fantasies in hard copy bills from century link. "why would you tell everyone? I was already up here, why wouldn't you wait? doesn't it make you sick? don't you just wanna die?"

"I wanna die because it drives me crazy! I wanna die because your mother left me! and it's just girlfriends, and it's women I buy handbags for, your mother got away, and you're perfect for me, and some guy, some fucking suit who's never met anyone honest gets mad at me making my own way, some greasy kid gets the pin when I worked you over, it drives me nuts! you know doctors can't save me. what are they supposed to do for you? they can't get to you. natural law is ultimate.

"what else would you be doing, you're a child."

I've done 12 good things this week for a bullet pop. boys watch my work, strain their eyes looking in their head at the overlay screen projection of porn onto our young bodies by our fathers, proud, in a dream that comes back to me. softcore dream most nights, I'm a child on my back, looking up at the kitchen as a dog would, and he's over me. he fucks me, and that's all this is about.

it's just a dream! and you laugh for me.

he only felt me up like I worked for him, and don't worry for me, hr will look into it.

good, good.

I get up. I look at the backyard, the grass grown out of bounds of vinyl rooting. tossed plastic from over the fence. burnt boxes that held rain from heaven, a type of firework, of fine needle, of light on the grass burning ends, absence, the sun setting. hr looked into it. there was nothing so vile I can't keep working.

that's alright. that's what he always said would happen. I don't lack for mental toughness. I turn to resume my work. I turn, see myself still under him, my body an intern, unpaid by either of us, she just suffers. she gets course credit! I turn back. we live in god's dream of god's needs, and god's desires, and shame. the loathing of your part, and the way you came without wanting to, is rejection of his light. "this can't be me, it just can't, have you ever been close to a hummingbird? I've done such beautiful things, it just can't.

"maybe if the head was of silicone, and separate, and penetrated, maybe, maybe."

oh god. this is great news for me.

oh god, this is great content.

oh god, fuck her! see what I care.

MONROE! WITH FORD MONROE (KTS, 1976)

S5.E29 (aired 4|15)

featuring marlon brando in support of THE MISSOURI BREAKS

MARLON:

it's not gonna stop.

[*MARLON looks himself over in the glass of the coffee table, bright with the tones necessary to make tv look good. his eyes aren't changing like he'd hoped they would. brando men take on this sort of glass eye look, you know, because you never see the eye move, it's just never on you. you'd walk around the whole room and he wouldn't look at you, his father. he figures he's reached a point of changing. too hot, or too cold, and he might come out a woman. he might be like this forever.*]

MARLON:

I think it's remorse.

MONROE:

I know you hate to hear it. I know you don't wanna answer. I just can't help but ask: how do you get the movies so real? what is it you do to accomplish that? that's what we're all after, marlon, we wanna know how you made it big!

[*the AUDIENCE claps, becomes a touch rowdy. MONROE runs a pretend comb through his hair.*]

MARLON:

more than I wanted dignity, or to love myself, I wanted relief. everybody's heard of it, haven't we?

[*MARLON makes big, "oh brother" gestures, and MONROE makes a smaller, inside, "this guy!" gesture for AUDIENCE. everyone claps polite for the trade of jabs, but what they really wanna see is a knockout.*]

MARLON:

you know what? I like you, monroe. I like you and your crowd. I'm gonna let you behind the curtain. hey, you know, actually, I can think of the three scenes that made me a capital-"A"-Actor. I need someone to join me onstage from the audience. monroe, I'd like you to just watch. really taste what you're feeling.

MARLON:

alright, now, one of you come on down and see me.

[*a MAN a little taller than MARLON stands, same build, just a hair taller, more imposing due to the numbers of it all, but not so scary you wouldn't let him up to your place at the end of the night, as he's given you no reason to distrust his athleticism, so it gives way to admiration, he could smash me up, isn't that hot? it's like he can take whatever he wants from me, but his manners, and gratitude for finishing in my mouth, and I make him nervous! can you believe! he's finally made it to the stage. his hair is white leaning to–*]

MARLON:

are you blond or premature gray?

MAN:

fuck if I know. I really don't care.

[*MARLON puts his hands up on the MAN's shoulders and they stay stiff, like he's never relaxed a day in his life.*]

MARLON:

you work out?

MAN:

I worked construction a while. I eat clean. you work out?

MARLON:

yeah, yeah, this is no accident.

[*MARLON turns away from the MAN, and gets down on his knees.*]

MARLON:

I want you to do whatever feels natural.

MAN:

I can do whatever to you?

MARLON:

if it feels natural to the character, absolutely. I trust you to know what's in character.

[*the MAN gets down behind MARLON. he runs his hands over MARLON's chest, pulling him back by the stomach. the MAN starts at MARLON'S buttons. MARLON moves the MAN'S hand over to his hip. the MAN feels out MARLON'S belt. the MAN starts to move center to the buckle.*]

MARLON:

over the slacks is tv. you've got to consider the medium. you don't do tv for film, for theater, you know. you will know, you've just never done tv before. whatever's natural—

[*the MAN presses down on the middle of MARLON'S back. he knocks the wind from MARLON'S chest. his ass stretches his dress slacks, the middle seam popping away from definition, unflattering visually, he must feel his way*] *out of this. he positions himself and presses down on the seam. MARLON is making some kind of noise, like he likes it, like it's hurting him and he can't pick. the AUDIENCE, MONROE, let him sound it out.*]

MARLON:

my mother met this young man at her job. she was only thirtysomething, but he was in his twenties. they'd been intimate, I realize now, but she always brought him up to me to call ugly. I never met the man, but that's the throughline. he was ugly, and he didn't deserve my mother, she said. one night she can't get ahold of him. she's calling and calling the bar and he won't pick up. "tell him it's me!" she's calling and calling and getting so angry. I was in middle school at the time, and I didn't have my own room. I believe she, my brother, and I shared the room. she says, "you talk, marlon!" she tells me to sound like a pretty girl. she puts me on the phone and I sound pretty, and I'm passed off to this young man. she takes the phone. "you've made a big mistake," she says. she slams the receiver and cries, "how could I let someone so ugly treat me like that?" she's asking me, I realize. I don't have an answer. "can't you just hug me?" I step outside my body and I hold her. I sit on the floor awhile, in my head, at the foot of the bed watching the middle of a movie—

MARLON:

sometimes you are compelled to move beyond the medium. sometimes tv isn't enough. tv is the lap, and, it's what we both want, to move beyond that. this is bringing on some sort of— fuck, I think we may be lost in the characters.

[*the MAN grips MARLON to bruises. he keeps asking for more, but the MAN has locked himself up on MARLON.*

this is plenty, this is a fantasy, and in a way, the whole fantasy of any actor is the generational role, the once-in-a-lifetime fuck, a scene that takes on history, and subsequent myth, and the seam of the pants running up his softest skin simulates the uterus taking the full force of a man, a strong man, up into its cervix. it's an issue of arousal that this happens, but the woman takes it because she's always believed herself to be in need of proper punishment. and all of this together feels as though, finally, man has conquered the divide between sexual pleasure and the awful child in every woman. MARLON remains nowhere near an orgasm, submitting, the pain a sort of quiet. it's been loud for so long, you'll take quiet however you can get it. and peace is a sort of quiet, a political quiet, that comes over us when everyone feels they've gotten just what they deserve. the MAN finishes, and rolls off MARLON, down on his back. MARLON stands, looking down over the MAN. the MAN is kicking off his wet pants and checking the pockets.]

MARLON:

would you like to know your name?

MAN:

it doesn't matter what you call me.

MARLON:

you're Richard then.

MAN:

I think you ought to get going. I've got an early day tomorrow.

[the MAN lays there. the MAN becomes RICHARD. the stage lights dim on him, and come up on MONROE. RICHARD smokes in the dark, feeling bad about how he's

presented himself. he thinks a lot about how good it felt to hurt MARLON, and how nice MARLON made him feel for doing it. someone's really broken him in, made him tough. and when you know you're tough, you can't help but test a guy. I can't, anyway. he wipes himself on the inside of his boxers and lays back on his hands. MARLON takes his seat beside MONROE.]

MARLON:

that was scene one. would you join me for scene two, monroe?

[the AUDIENCE claps, and MONROE blushes. he chuckles, and swings a bat in pretend. home run!]

MONROE:

sure marlon, I'd love an oscar!

[clapping, clapping.]

MARLON:

for this next scene, you'll be my father.

[AUDIENCE makes a flirty sort of noise, a voyeuristic encouragement of onstage play.]

MONROE:

I'll be your daddy, marlon.

[AUDIENCE hoots, starts getting warm.]

MARLON:

you're already doing wonderful. sexual excitement is a core part of the character's motivation in almost any scene. that you've keyed into that immediately is big, not only for your interpretation, but mine as "MARLON." we are to be in a room together. that is imperative to the experience of my father, physical presence. he's sort of shy over the phone.

MONROE:

I'm not shy, I'm smart. I don't wanna be monitored.

MARLON:

you really think like a father, monroe, I hope you have kids of your own someday.

MONROE:

I hope they look just like you, marlon.

[*MARLON tightens up in his chair, covering his genitals with his hands, his kicked over leg. it's not that he's aroused by his father, but rather his father impersonates strangers when speaking to him. things that a father should never say become sort of—routine, unscrubbed of sex, dirty and filling the vein, inducing a sort of erotic sepsis. thank god he's just pulp of this book, of this physical book which you can sell for not a cash profit but a moral one.*]

MARLON:

are the olympics over yet? I can't speak to my mother until after the olympics, and even yesterday is too soon but I realize I've made agreements I need to keep. it's my pleasure to keep, dad.

MONROE:

the olympics ended last week.

MARLON:

we'd watch an event, and then she'd go around the room and compare everyone's bodies to the athletes'.

MONROE:

how did you size up, marlon?

MARLON:

poorly. I size up great next to the dallas cheerleaders.

MONROE:

I don't know what you mean by that.

MARLON:

I can't tell you how your wife works, dad.

MARLON:

now, monroe, that was smart of me to say. my father would never put up with that from me. I want you to get up like you want to scare me.

[*MONROE stands, his chair tips back loudly. MARLON jumps at the sound in a small way, some clenched teeth, and then his face goes idle. no one takes MONROE for a tough guy, not even these actor types. he wanted to take MARLON'S body and juice it like an orange. he wanted to shut him up, to stop throbbing against his zipper.*]

MONROE:

how am I supposed to feel about this?

MARLON:

I don't know, but I'll hand you the facts from my father: I am beautiful. what's it usually feel like to be up against something beautiful? here—

[*MARLON turns his head, makes himself flat against the wall. MONROE comes up into his neck. he and MARLON touch shirts. MONROE has an empty smile, like a dog's standing over another bowing dog. the audience hoots and hollers, and whistles, and cheers for MONROE, this moment to surely make the tape set sold after MONROE dies, the ad between phone sex and the back of some cab with three girls getting in. this is a moment! now just stick it, MARLON, and I'll cum–*]

MONROE:

whoa, hey, I'm retiring! I'm retiring from acting!

[*AUDIENCE claps!*]

MARLON:

follow that instinct.

[*AUDIENCE laughs and claps!*]

MONROE:

yeah, well what if I–

[*MONROE takes his thumb and wipes hard past MARLON'S chest, the nipple getting stiff and seen through the breast of his shirt. MONROE wants to put his mouth on it, but fears the audience may turn. what's happened before this was playful. this act, too, could pass for play, if you know the psychology of an audience like I, a father, MONROE, only can.*]

WOMAN:

monroe!

[*WOMAN, MARLON'S mother, a yet uncasted role, cries because she knows what she saw, but this is MONROE. MARLON can't see her past the lights.*]

MARLON:

I'm alright.

[*AUDIENCE claps, more satisfied-leaning. the presumed heart of the episode.*]

MONROE:

you'd do that for me?

[*MONROE lets MARLON by to the center of the set. MARLON holds his chest.*]

MARLON:

I've got no control over it, but it feels obscene to show. this is how fast you've gotta be going from one emotion from the next. if you asked me to cry, I could cry. I could pivot into arousal. when we get these mixed signals from loved ones, we see it as a fork in the road. to act, you must see it as a highway extension, and the cars are the lifeblood of experience. we need traffic. I'd never know how to get off without traffic.

MARLON:

thank you, dad. alright, I'll call my mother now.

[*MARLON sits in his chair, and brings his hand up to his ear like a phone.*]

MARLON:

mother? right, whoever that was, would you?

[*a WOMAN stands and comes down from the third row, a capri pant, a sweater of uncharacteristically close robins over water. she's tight on the railing. she sits beside MARLON, her hand to her ear.*]

MARLON:

mom?

WOMAN:

yes, son?

MARLON:

dad's been talking about trapping eagles in mexico with his brother. he says it'd be easy to turn a profit.

WOMAN:

he just talks—

MARLON:

you ever see an eagle pick something up? they break up like ground beef.

WOMAN:

marlon, don't be morbid.

MARLON:

I'm scared for him, mom. I'm scared an eagle is gonna kill my dad. that's stupid, mom, it's a stupid problem to have. and he's talking about keeping cages here at the house. what if he gets one? then there's an eagle in my house, it's fucking stupid—

WOMAN:

are you cussing at me, marlon?

MARLON:

jesus—

WOMAN:

well, are you?

MARLON:

jesus christ, mom, I'm not cussing at you! I'm scared!

WOMAN:

you know he just talks.

MARLON:

okay.

WOMAN:

don't get short with me.

[*MARLON strikes himself in the thigh. AUDIENCE gasps. the WOMAN holds her mouth. he strikes again and again until he doubles over. he holds his leg, his face away from the phone. his eyes start to take on water.*]

MARLON:

don't look at me. I'm at home, you can't see me.

[*the WOMAN looks away. his face softens, and all the red runs out, giving way to a healthy tan.*]

MARLON:

I know he just talks.

[*AUDIENCE claps. this is acting!*]

WOMAN:

don't worry so much. you've always tried to carry everything for everyone. you deserve to be light.

MARLON:

thank you, mom.

MARLON:

something happened tonight, mom.

MARLON:

my dad—your husband—is attracted to me, and he's made his feelings known to me. why do you think this has happened? your answer is very important to me, so take all the time you need.

WOMAN:

I don't know much about you, marlon. not like I know your father, monroe. I know, just from watching, as someone who loves you, you're awful flirtatious.

MARLON:

was I flirtatious tonight?

WOMAN:

if I was scared of my father, I wouldn't go back and forth like you do. you're just getting him all riled up and you're expecting someone to come save you.

MARLON:

should children not expect protection?

WOMAN:

you weren't a child, marlon, this just happened moments ago.

MARLON:

mom, I told you, this isn't the first time. he's wanted me as long as I can remember.

WOMAN:

why didn't you tell me then? what am I supposed to do now with this?

MARLON:

you're supposed to be sick for me! I'm supposed to talk you out of coming down to the studio with a gun!

WOMAN:

that's sick, marlon, this is my husband were talking about! he's my best friend. he's been there for me since before I knew you. I'll always love him.

MARLON:

yeah, well, that's sick. that's disgusting, and you ought to get yourself checked out.

[*MARLON holds his palm over the mouthpiece. he nods MONROE over. they sit cross-legged on the floor opposite one another. MARLON'S mother watches them from her seat. they are to practice another acting technique: automatic arousal. should an actor be presented with some sexual content, political content, violent content by which he cannot abide, he simply becomes someone else who can. if he cannot tolerate his father's touch as his son, he becomes his woman.*]

WOMAN:

he was always so gracious with you, marlon, it's just a shock to be hearing this is all. that something so horrible was happening and you just told no one.

[*MONROE leans back on his hands.*]

MONROE:

I want you to come over, marlon, is that sick?

MARLON:

it's in character.

[*MARLON sits on MONROE's lap, balancing his weight on his heels. MONROE kicks his feet out, and MARLON tips. he catches himself. MONROE lays back on the floor, rubs circles in MARLON'S back.*]

MONROE:

how old would you be?

MARLON:

that's an excellent question. I'd say I was, at most, 12. I do believe there's some component of humiliation, on my part, to the act. so you get hard, every pervert can do that. you call your kid over at his birthday party and make him sit?

MONROE:

it's power. you really are the stuff of dreams, marlon. if I wasn't your father, there'd be heavy stuff between you and I.

[*MARLON'S heels start to burn, the arches get sharp.*]

MARLON:

it's time to dismiss me, monroe, we've got all these people here. someone might object.

[*MARLON stands. he walks back over to his chair, picks up the receiver.*]

MARLON:

mom?

[*the WOMAN holds her mouth like she's gonna hurl. she won't look up at MARLON.*]

MARLON:

mom? I don't want you to hate me—

WOMAN:

I don't hate you, marlon, I just don't know what to say.

MARLON:

you know, I've thought a lot about what I'd wanna hear. I'm not gonna make you do anything. we can just start healing now, mom. you didn't seem ready to hear how things were just yet, and I think it's best we don't make a big deal of things. we needed dad, even after we left, and I understand, and I'm not asking for anything.

WOMAN:

I'm sorry I couldn't meet all your needs as a single mother.

MARLON:

that's okay.

WOMAN:

you just had it so bad. you got to follow your dreams, marlon! I had all my kids before you even won an oscar!

MARLON:

I'm not asking you for anything!

[*the WOMAN stands.*]

WOMAN:

when you talk like that it makes me want to hit you in the mouth.

MARLON:

I'm not scared of you, mom. I could really hurt you, mom, but I don't want to.

[*the WOMAN stands, her hands balled up at her sides. she twists her mouth, leaning in her shoulder like she'll swing from the hip. she stands, over MARLON now. it was effective for his father. and he's never listened to me, but he was scared of him, so then all of a sudden he can hear. MARLON looks away from his mother, leans back on his palms. deferment! this, too, is acting! AUDIENCE claps. she settles down into her seat.*]

MARLON:

I'd kill you, mom. I'd feel horrible.

WOMAN:

you don't know what I can do.

MARLON:

that's fantastic stuff. that's just like my mother.

WOMAN:

why do you sometimes call me mom, and sometimes call me mother?

MARLON:

all you have to say is you can't stand him either. you don't see him. you don't want to. you see me, mom. how can you stand him, haven't you listened to any of this? his idea of retirement was me in his lap full time. I don't get married, I don't have kids, I just get him off all day. that's all he wanted for me. I wish he was dead, mom, that's why I did that movie. it wasn't hard to see myself doing something awful to him.

WOMAN:

you're sick, marlon.

MARLON:

Richard only hurt me! he said he'd fuck my kid, so we didn't have any! it's as easy as that!

WOMAN:

your father would never say anything like that to someone he loved.

MARLON:

no, he'd just go ahead and fuck me. and then he'd buy me a video game. Richard is the only one who's ever been honest with me about what was happening, even when it made me sick.

WOMAN:

so you want your dad to talk nasty to you?

[*the WOMAN stands out of her chair to center. she throws up her arms to say "get real." they laugh. she throws them up again.*]

WOMAN:

I mean?

[*she keeps throwing as long as they clap. MARLON gets himself calm. this is not a satisfying end to the work. she knows it too. this is meant to change the momentum of the scene. the scene can't all be one thing, never, ever. no one remembers it. if you don't intend to stick, why get all these people together and waste their fucking time? the scene's got to swing the other way. I have lost control of my temper, and I'm being crass to shock her. when it's just us two, sure,*]

I get a kick out of it. but all these people are turned off now, thinking of me, a child beneath MONROE. this is a lose-lose. I am GEORGE on the side of the road walking home to MARTHA, and what's-his-name that she fucks. I think his name is also GEORGE. it's either I've been crass, or you don't look like a kid. that's what they'd say if I could come in 12. they think it's a compliment. either way, I've gotten myself worked up. I've been teaching myself chess, and this has been a reoccurring problem. you tell me what I'm supposed to do, and I do it. I don't think much of how. I'm all instinct. it gets me picked apart. she doesn't like the how, so she's the victim. I'm just sitting here talking myself into a fit. she's just some lady. aren't we all!

AUDIENCE sits quiet, hands in their laps. the WOMAN stops throwing.]

WOMAN:

marlon. [*winded, fanning the shoulders of her sweater, the robins on choppy air.*] you asked me why I thought this happened. I told you, and I have been attacked, and attacked. what are you after?

MARLON:

do you still love my father?

WOMAN:

I've never met your father.

MARLON:

do you still love monroe then? would you tell me to show him kindness?

[*the WOMAN stands, and kisses MARLON on the forehead.*]

WOMAN:

oh marlon. oh marlon, how do I put this—it's like we're all mary tyler moore, he's dick van dyke, and you're just, well, *turn-on*.

[*MARLON hides his face in his palm, pressing the skin of the middle red, and his eyes ache. he brings down his wet hand, wet with sweat, wet with crying, and wipes it on his pants.*]

WOMAN:

oh marlon, did I ever tell you how your father and I used to watch movies together? we'd get loaded on malt liquor and watch *the mack*! we would laugh and laugh—

[*the WOMAN and MONROE get down to the carpet on one side to smile at the other's potential: kids are a crapshoot. I know I can make you perfect for me.*

over on the dark side of the stage, RICHARD lays in a hall light. he spits on his hands and works on himself, picturing his fuck squatting over him, standing up out of the pain when it gets to be too much, only to come back down again. it'd really turn me on if you came down again.

MARLON comes over, comes out of his suit into scene three.]

RICHARD:

most times, to fuck just one person, I need some kind of flick on of whatever I don't have but you, marlon—

RICHARD:

oh—

RICHARD:

just come down already.

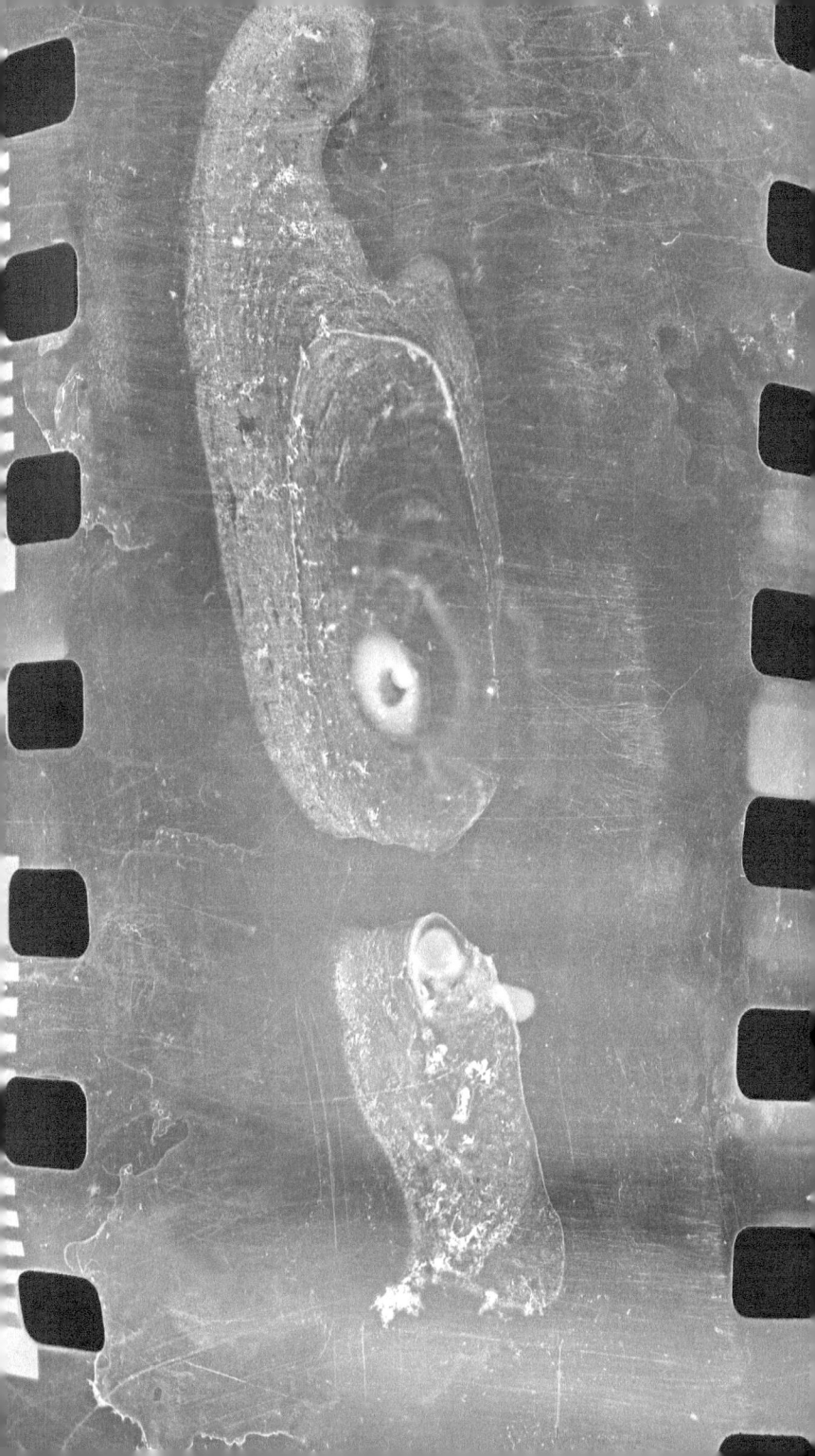

WORKS CITED

[1] MORTENSEN, VIGGO. *Screen Tests*. "*on Meryl Streep, Marlon Brando...*". *W Magazine*. "https://www.youtube.com/watch?v=Yd8L_L8mlEo", *2017*.

[2] HAMMER, ARMAND DOUGLAS (ALLEGED). "'House of Hammer'...". *Variety. 2022*.

[3] MENENDEZ, ERIK. *Secret Lives: The Menendez Brothers*. CNN. 2014.

[4] PIPER, RODDY. *Timeline: 1984—As Told by Piper, R. Kayfabe Commentaries. 2014.*

[5] BRANDO, MARLON. *Last Tango in Paris. PEA. Les Productions Artistes Associés. 1972.*

[6] MCMAHON, VINCENT K. *Grant v. World Wrestling Entertainment, inc et al (3:24-cv-00090), Connecticut District Court. Exhibit 168. 2024.*

[7] BRANDO, MARLON. *A Streetcar Named Desire. Warner Bros. 1951.*

[8] CAVETT, DICK. *The Dick Cavett Show*. "June 12, 1973". ABC. 1973.

[9] BRANDO, MARLON. *The Dick Cavett Show*. "June 12, 1973". ABC. 1973.

[10] KEMPER, EDMUND. "Murder: No Apparent Motive". *Rainbow Broadcasting Co. 1984.*

[11] SOLOMON. *Ecclesiastes 2:10. New King James Version.*

ACKNOWLEDGMENTS

"MUSIC NO.00 'AND HIS BANNER OVER ME WAS LOVE'" was first published as *AND HIS BANNER OVER ME WAS LOVE* by Pansy Press in 2024.

"MONTGOMERY CLIFT AS WESTERN PLEASURE IN *years from now you'll be glad you did this*" was first published as "YEARS FROM NOW YOU'LL BE GLAD YOU DID THIS" by *The Poetry Project Newsletter* (Issue #273, edited by Saretta Morgan).

the-end-